HOW TO DRAW DINOSAURS, GH LETTERING & SPACECRAFT

Part One
HOW TO DRAW DINOSAURS AND PREHISTORIC LIFE

Marit Claridge

Consultant:
John Shackell

Edited by Judy Tatchell
Designed by Mike Pringle and Richard Johnson

**Illustrated by Val Biro,
Philip Hood and John Shackell**

Contents

About part one

Millions of years ago, monstrous dinosaurs and strange mammals ruled the earth. They are fun to draw because although there are some clues to what they looked like, nobody can be exactly sure.

Drawing around skeletons

Dinosaurs died out millions of years before humans appeared. The only clues to how they looked come from parts of their skeletons which have been found preserved in rock. These remains are called fossils. People called paleontologists piece the fossils together, working out how the missing bits of skeleton might have looked.

Look out for pictures of dinosaur skeletons in books, which you can trace round, as shown here. Remember to leave space for the missing muscles and flesh.

Small bones are supported by small muscles, so the outline is close to the bones here.

Big bones need strong muscles to support them, so leave plenty of space for muscle here.

Colouring dinosaurs

Nobody knows exactly what colours the dinosaurs were. Most were probably similar to the trees and ferns around them.

Paleontologists base their colour guesses on the reptiles and plants alive today. You, however, can colour them as brightly as you wish.

Drawing styles

In this book you can find out how to draw realistic-looking prehistoric animals as well as cartoon characters. You can also find out how to draw cartoon cave people.

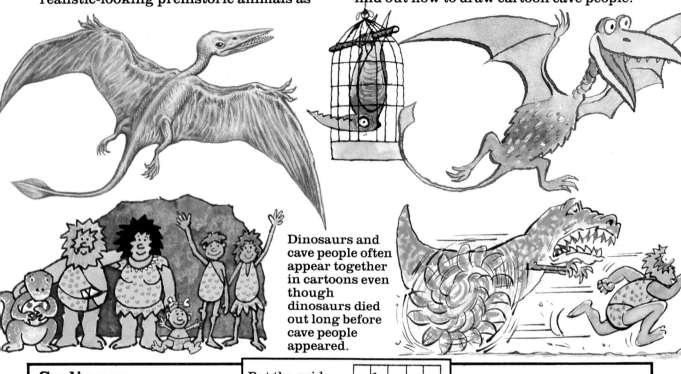

Dinosaurs and cave people often appear together in cartoons even though dinosaurs died out long before cave people appeared.

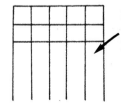

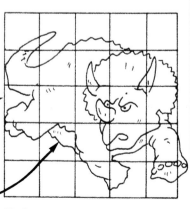

Scaling up

You can learn a lot about how to draw prehistoric life by copying the illustrations in this book. If you want to make your drawing bigger than the one in the book, you can scale up the illustration using a grid.

Draw a grid on tracing paper made up of equal-sized squares.

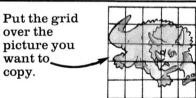

Put the grid over the picture you want to copy.

Draw another light pencil grid on a piece of drawing paper. Use the same number of squares but twice the size of those on the tracing grid, to double the size of the picture.

Look at the squares laid on top of the picture. Copy the shapes in each one into the same square on the drawing paper grid.

Rub out the grid lines when you have inked the outline.

Shapes and colours

On these two pages there are tips on how to draw and colour prehistoric animals. You may find these techniques useful later in the book.

Simple shapes

Prehistoric deer

1

2

3

However complicated an animal looks, it is made up of simpler shapes. Throughout the book there are line drawings which show how to build up the animals using simple shapes. Draw the red lines first, then the blue and then the green.

Colours

Many of the animals in the book are coloured using watercolour paints. Some of the colours have unusual names. These are explained in **Artist's colours** boxes.

A paintbox with a large range of colours should have all the colours you need. You can also buy tubes of watercolours in any colour you wish.

Artist's colours
Ochre is a pale brownish yellow.

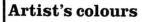

Washes

A wash is a thin coat of watery paint. When you colour a large animal, mix up plenty of the wash colour in a separate container.

4

Skin textures

Dinosaurs had thick, leathery skins like elephants, or dry, warty skins. You can use the tips below to paint and crayon the skins of the dinosaurs in this book.

Dry, warty skin

 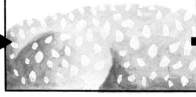 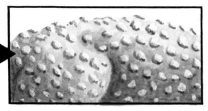

Colour the area with a light to medium wash. When dry, add a second, darker layer to the shaded areas.

Cover the area with thick white spots. Mix some wash colour with the white to darken the spots in the shaded areas.

Add dark shadows beneath the spots and draw extra dark lines beneath the body to strengthen the shadows.

Using a sponge

Thick, leathery skin

  or

For another warty skin, begin with a wash, as before. Then dip a small sponge in a darker mix of paint and dab it gently over the area.

Begin with a background wash. When dry, draw dark, heavy lines where the body creases. Add highlights with dry, white paint.

With crayons and pencils, colour the dinosaur with the paper resting on a rough surface, such as sandpaper, cement or grainy wood.

Artist's tip

Some of the prehistoric creatures in this book are two-legged. A common problem when drawing them is that they can look off balance. This makes them appear weak.

To make them balance, there must be as much weight in front of their legs as behind. Draw a vertical line and build your animal up around it.

Weight too far back.

Weight too far forward.

Draw equal amounts of the animal's bulk either side of the line.

Line shows where the animal's weight is falling.

Heads and tails

The dinosaurs on these two pages have strange heads or tails and odd bodies.

These make them fun to draw and ideal for turning into cartoons.

Stegosaurus

Use a darker shade for the far plates and far legs. This makes them look further away.

Plates

The head hangs low as the front legs are shorter than the back legs.

Sketch the basic shape of the Stegosaurus (pronounced Steg-oh-saw-rus) in pencil. Begin with the body, then add the neck, head, tail and legs. Draw the plates last.

To colour the Stegosaurus, use the techniques shown on page 5 for dry warty skin on the body and thick leathery skin around the legs.

Ankylosaurus

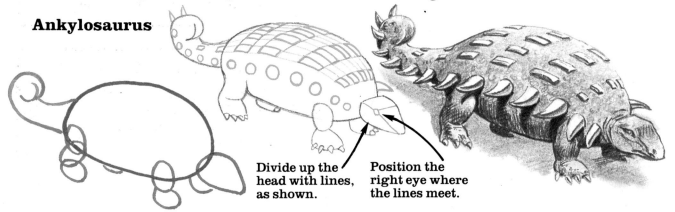

Divide up the head with lines, as shown.

Position the right eye where the lines meet.

Above are the basic shapes for an Ankylosaurus (pronounced An-kil-oh-saw-rus).

Draw faint circles along the body to position the body spikes and curved lines to position the back plates.

Add spikes and back plates. Leave white highlights on them. Add strong shadows under the spikes and body.

Crested dinosaurs

Some dinosaurs had crests on their heads which probably helped them recognize each other. The crests had air passages inside which meant the dinosaurs could make loud, bellowing calls. These crests may have been very colourful.

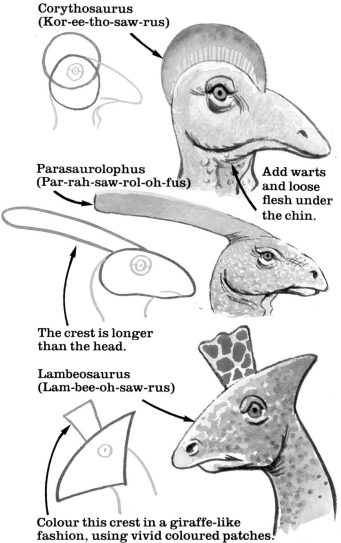

Corythosaurus
(Kor-ee-tho-saw-rus)

Add warts and loose flesh under the chin.

Parasaurolophus
(Par-rah-saw-rol-oh-fus)

The crest is longer than the head.

Lambeosaurus
(Lam-bee-oh-saw-rus)

Colour this crest in a giraffe-like fashion, using vivid coloured patches.

Cartoon dinosaurs

The Ankylosaurus used the bone at the end of its tail as a club to fend off meat-eaters. Try copying this cartoon which makes fun of the situation.

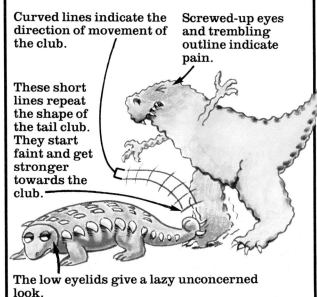

Curved lines indicate the direction of movement of the club.

Screwed-up eyes and trembling outline indicate pain.

These short lines repeat the shape of the tail club. They start faint and get stronger towards the club.

The low eyelids give a lazy unconcerned look.

Make your own monster

You could try mixing up some of the heads, tails and bodies on these pages to make your own imaginary monster.

A vegetarian giant

The Diplodocus (Dip-loh-doh-kus) was the longest dinosaur. It measured 27m (89ft) from nose to tail – about as long as a tennis court.

Use a darker, thicker mix of the wash colour for the shadows under the body.

Wrinkles

Shade under the body and neck and in the curve of the tail.

Draw in wrinkles around the legs and where the tail and neck bend.

Colour the far legs a darker shade.

Draw the oval body shape first. Then add the long neck and tail and the heavy legs.

The Diplodocus had thick, leathery skin, like an elephant. Colour it with shades of green watercolour using the technique shown on page 5.

Turn your animal around

A simple plasticine model can be a great help if you want to draw your Diplodocus from different angles.

Mold some plasticine into seven pieces – the body, neck, tail and four legs. Press the pieces together to form your model. Keep it small or the neck will be too heavy to stand out from the body. You could stand the model on a small piece of cardboard so that you can move it easily.

Shadows on the body help to make the animal look heavy and solid. Shine a lamp or torch at your model so that you can see where the shadows fall.

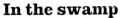

In the swamp

The Diplodocus lived in swamps. Try drawing a wet, glossy Diplodocus in a prehistoric swamp.

Paint simple leaf shapes.

Less detail in distant trees.

White highlights make the skin look wet.

Use darker shades below.

Steam rising.

Let colours run together.

Keep near edges sharp.

Use muddy browns for the water.

Add touches of blue to reflect the sky.

Get a swampy water effect by taking wiggly lines from roots and stems.

Draw the outline of the Diplodocus and tree trunks in pencil. Paint ferns and trees with plenty of creepers. Colour the trees and water with very wet washes. While the paint is still damp, dab some of the colour away with tissue. This gives the effect of steam rising. Colour the Diplodocus as before.

A worm's eye view

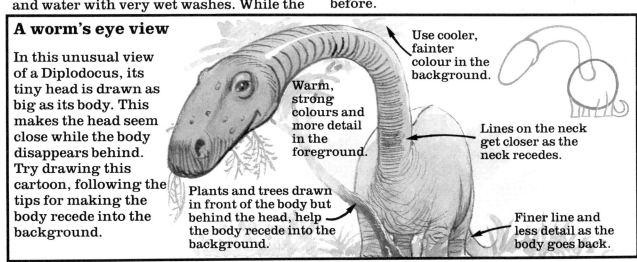

In this unusual view of a Diplodocus, its tiny head is drawn as big as its body. This makes the head seem close while the body disappears behind. Try drawing this cartoon, following the tips for making the body recede into the background.

Use cooler, fainter colour in the background.

Warm, strong colours and more detail in the foreground.

Lines on the neck get closer as the neck recedes.

Plants and trees drawn in front of the body but behind the head, help the body recede into the background.

Finer line and less detail as the body goes back.

Sea monsters

At the time of the dinosaurs, the seas were the home of huge creatures. These two pages show you how to draw three sea monsters in a dramatic scene above and below the water.

Indigo fades to pale yellow underneath.

Add white highlights for a glossy wet skin.

For sharp-looking teeth, draw a row of triangles. Paint them white against a dark mouth.

Fade the sea colour and draw the waves smaller and fainter towards the horizon. This helps make the distant sea look further away.

Draw a sharp outline above the water.

Ichthyosaurus
(Ik-thi-oh-saw-rus)

Artist's colours

Indigo is a very dark blue.

Outline fades underwater. Blend with sea water colour.

Elasmosaurus
(Ee-laz-mo-saw-rus)

Animal shapes

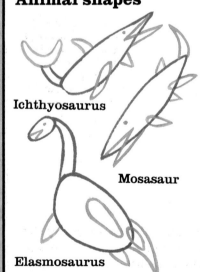

Ichthyosaurus

Mosasaur

Elasmosaurus

Scaly skin

The Mosasaur has scaly skin, like a crocodile. Use a wash of greeny browns and greys. When the paint is dry, use a thin brush, sharp crayon or a fine dark felt tip to draw the scaly ridges. Add white highlights to make it look wet and shiny.

Long white highlight makes fish look wet.

For fish, use shades of blue, green and yellow. Start dark at the top and fade to pale yellow beneath. Criss-cross with fine black lines.

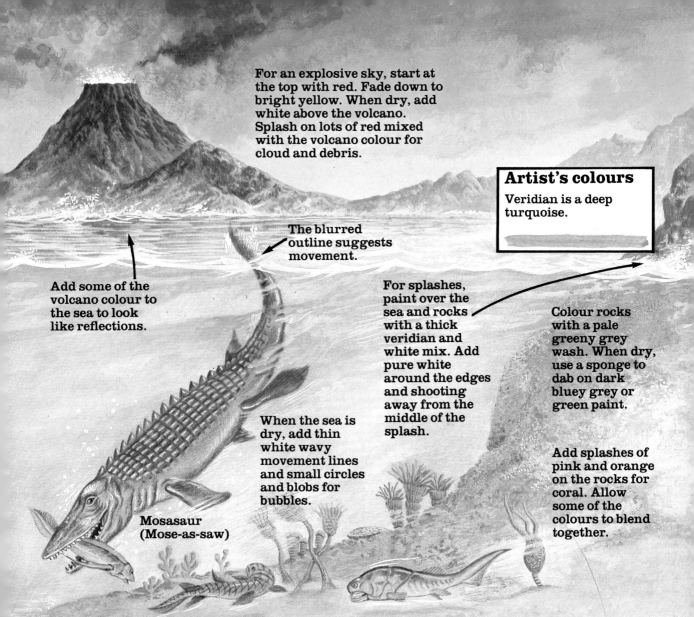

For an explosive sky, start at the top with red. Fade down to bright yellow. When dry, add white above the volcano. Splash on lots of red mixed with the volcano colour for cloud and debris.

The blurred outline suggests movement.

Artist's colours

Veridian is a deep turquoise.

Add some of the volcano colour to the sea to look like reflections.

For splashes, paint over the sea and rocks with a thick veridian and white mix. Add pure white around the edges and shooting away from the middle of the splash.

Colour rocks with a pale greeny grey wash. When dry, use a sponge to dab on dark bluey grey or green paint.

When the sea is dry, add thin white wavy movement lines and small circles and blobs for bubbles.

Add splashes of pink and orange on the rocks for coral. Allow some of the colours to blend together.

Mosasaur (Mose-as-saw)

Under the sea

First colour the monsters, coral and underwater rocks. Leave these to dry. Then cover the whole area with a veridian wash. When this dries, add wavy lines of darker veridian across the picture. Paint darker veridian lines alongside the Mosasaur too. These help to make the creature look as if it is moving through the sea.

Flying creatures

Above the dinosaurs the skies were ruled by large flying reptiles, called pterosaurs. Here you can find out how to draw two different types as well as a strip cartoon about an Archaeopteryx, the first real bird.

Pteranodon

Draw a faint dotted line and use this to position the body, legs and arms. Add the wings, neck and head.

Add shadows and veins in dark brown.

Paint the Pteranodon (Ter-a-no-don) with a thin grey wash. When dry, go over it again with a thin pinky brown wash.

Use a thick mix of the pinky brown colour for highlights.

Follow the tips on pages 10 and 11 for colouring the sea and rocks.

Artist's tip

You can save time by using a hairdrier to dry the wash.

Archaeopteryx

The Archaeopteryx (Ark-ee-op-ter-iks) used its sharp claws to climb trees and its wings to glide. It was too heavy to fly and its beak full of teeth would have made it nose-heavy.

Try copying this strip cartoon about an Archaeopteryx.

Beads of sweat show effort.

Draw the outline and feathers in black felt tip. Colour the bird with bright crayons or felt tips.

Wide eyes, curved brows and gaping mouth suggest mounting panic.

Bird's eye view

Animals and trees look quite different from above. The parts of the body that are nearer to you look bigger than those that are further away.

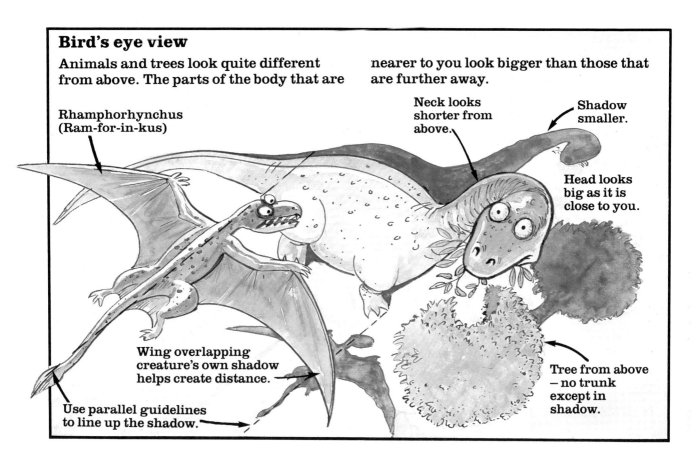

Rhamphorhynchus (Ram-for-in-kus)

Neck looks shorter from above.

Shadow smaller.

Head looks big as it is close to you.

Wing overlapping creature's own shadow helps create distance.

Tree from above – no trunk except in shadow.

Use parallel guidelines to line up the shadow.

Lines show direction of movement

Radiating lines make the impact look more dramatic.

CRUNCH

Extra beads of sweat suggest greater effort.

Dinosaur characters

People write stories about dinosaurs and prehistoric times because of the excitement of the unknown. All that remains of these creatures are their skeletons. The rest has to be made up. This mixture of reality and fantasy makes them ideal subjects for stories.

The dinosaurs on the next four pages are drawn in a cartoon story-book style. They are given characters, like people in a story.

Tyrannosaurus rex

The Tyrannosaurus rex (Tie-ran-oh-saw-rus rex) or T.rex was the biggest meat eater that ever lived. Its head alone was 1.5m (5ft) long – big enough to swallow a man whole.

Try painting the fierce T.rex below using masking fluid* to give its colourful skin a bumpy texture. You can also use this technique for the Triceratops on the next page and other dinosaurs with scaly skin.

Dot masking fluid on back.

Masking fluid lines on stomach and tail.

Copy or trace the T.rex. Paint on the masking fluid with a paper clip – do not use a brush or you will ruin it.

Green for back.

Yellow and orange for stomach.

When the masking fluid is dry, colour in the T. rex with watercolour.

White marks left behind by masking fluid.

When dry, rub off the masking fluid with your fingers. This will leave white marks.

Paint over the whole dinosaur with light washes of different colours to make colourful skin marks.

You can buy masking fluid from art material shops.

Triceratops

This brave, charging Triceratops (Try-ser-a-tops) was a fierce, plant-eating dinosaur. Its huge frilled head, three horns and strange beaked mouth help to give it a lot of character. Trace or copy the Triceratops here and colour it with orange, yellow and brown watercolour.

Add extra, soft markings with coloured crayons.

A timid T. rex

In most pictures the T. rex is shown as terrible and frightening. This T. rex is given a timid character. It looks alarmed — as it may have been if charged at by the heavily armoured Triceratops.

The down-turned mouth and backward looking eyes give the T. rex a worried expression.

Here it is running away. The staring eyes, slightly opened mouth and turned head make it look even more alarmed than before.

More dinosaur characters

The dinosaurs in this prehistoric scene are running from a fierce Tyrannosaurus rex. The artist makes the most of each dinosaur's special features to give the characters extra life. Copy the characters and try to change the expressions around using the tips given here.

The Diplodocus would have had little defence against the T.rex. Her dilated, turned-back eyes and down-turned mouth make the Diplodocus look frightened.

The frowning eyes and down-turned mouth make this Ankylosaurus look angry at being chased.

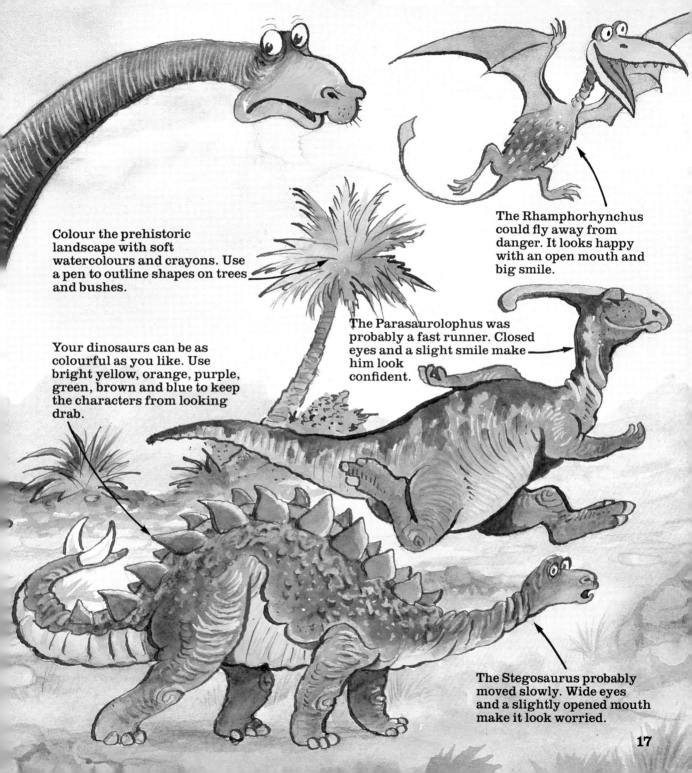

Colour the prehistoric landscape with soft watercolours and crayons. Use a pen to outline shapes on trees and bushes.

The Rhamphorhynchus could fly away from danger. It looks happy with an open mouth and big smile.

Your dinosaurs can be as colourful as you like. Use bright yellow, orange, purple, green, brown and blue to keep the characters from looking drab.

The Parasaurolophus was probably a fast runner. Closed eyes and a slight smile make him look confident.

The Stegosaurus probably moved slowly. Wide eyes and a slightly opened mouth make it look worried.

17

Cave people

On these two pages you can see how to draw a family of cave people.

Caveman and woman

Use the same basic shape for both the caveman and cavewoman.

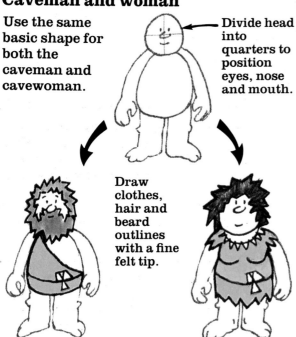

Divide head into quarters to position eyes, nose and mouth.

Draw clothes, hair and beard outlines with a fine felt tip.

Colour the clothes with yellow felt tip. Use a brown felt tip for the spots.

Jagged line looks like a tooth necklace.

A touch of grey on lower edge of axe head makes axe look more solid.

Add hairy arms and legs with a pencil.

Cave children

Use a pear shaped body for a boy or girl.

Divide head into equal quarters to position eyes and nose.

Thinner arms and legs than for adults.

Colour leopard skin clothes as before.

Add skirt to bottom of pear-shaped body.

Cave baby

The younger the child, the larger the head in proportion to the body.

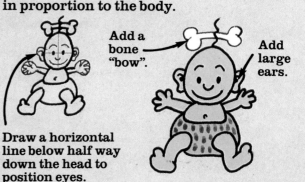

Add a bone "bow".

Add large ears.

Draw a horizontal line below half way down the head to position eyes.

18

Turning around

You can use the same basic body shapes to draw the cave children and adults from the front, back and side.

For a back view, turn feet away and fill head completely with hair colour.

For a three-quarter view, move facial features to left or right. Add the nose in profile. Change the arms and legs as shown.

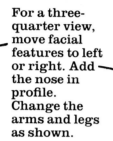

The side-on caveman in this cartoon is drawn starting with the same body shape as for a front view. You only have to alter the arm and leg positions and draw the face in profile.

Here you can see how colouring just the relevant part of the picture makes the point of the joke stand out.

Cave family at home

This cartoon shows some tricks you can use to make your pictures lively.

Leg breaks out to give impression of running into the picture.

For the blotchy effect, apply the paint with a sponge. Add more paint with a brush in darker areas.

Lines repeat tail shape.

Clouds of dust help to show speed.

Dust where ball bounces.

Cave paintings

Cave people painted pictures of animals such as horses and bison on the walls of their caves. The paintings on this page are copies of real cave paintings.

Copy the shapes and follow the colouring tips for realistic looking cave paintings.

The wall

You can achieve a realistic looking rock wall by putting a sheet of rough sandpaper under your paper. Colour the wall by rubbing fairly hard with crayons or pastels. The wall on the right is coloured in this way.

You can also use watercolours, as in the rest of the page. Use watery washes of soft colours. Apply the colours in patches, adding extra paint on joins to create angles.

For this effect, use crayons over sandpaper.

Colours

Cave people ground down soft, coloured rocks to make their paints. They would have used colours like the ones below.

Yellow   Yellow ochre   Red ochre   Raw sienna   Burnt sienna

Burnt umber   Black   Greys   White

This bison was coloured with paint dabbed on with a finger.

Pick out horns in white.

Use a few single brush strokes for the horse.

Changing faces

Cartoons are often made funny by the expressions on the characters' faces.

There are tips on how to draw different expressions throughout the book. Here are some more for you to practise.

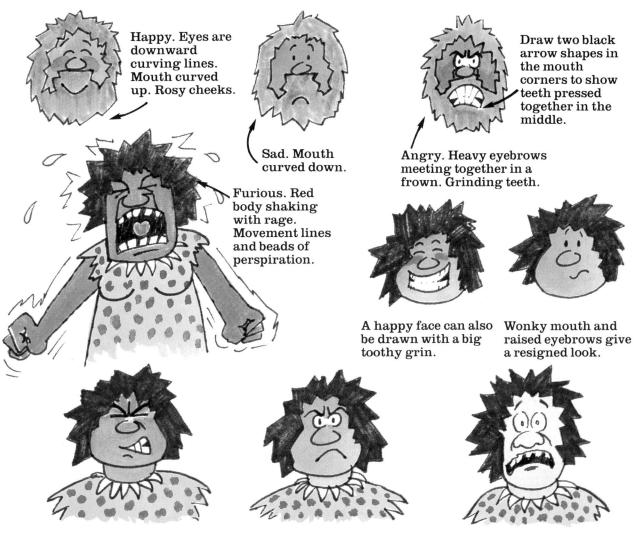

Happy. Eyes are downward curving lines. Mouth curved up. Rosy cheeks.

Sad. Mouth curved down.

Draw two black arrow shapes in the mouth corners to show teeth pressed together in the middle.

Angry. Heavy eyebrows meeting together in a frown. Grinding teeth.

Furious. Red body shaking with rage. Movement lines and beads of perspiration.

A happy face can also be drawn with a big toothy grin.

Wonky mouth and raised eyebrows give a resigned look.

Pain. Eyes screwed up tight. Red face. Mouth open one side only showing grinding teeth.

Downturned mouth and frowning eyes give a displeased expression.

Frightened. A green face with wide staring eyes, raised eyebrows and a quaking mouth.

Dinosaur strip cartoons

A strip cartoon is a funny story told in more than one picture. Each picture is within a frame with speech and thought added in bubbles. Try to make your characters look the same in each frame. It helps if you give them distinct features such as a big nose or beard.

Artist's tip

You can turn the characters of your strip cartoon around with the help of tracing paper. This works for side-views and three-quarter views. Trace the figure and simply turn the tracing over for the opposite view.

The tracing is like a mirror image where everything is reversed. If your character has clothes off one shoulder or a club in one hand, this has to be reversed back again.

Speech bubbles

You can add speech and thought to your story in bubbles. Use capital letters and keep the speech short. You can also add sound effects, which you can find out about on page 24.

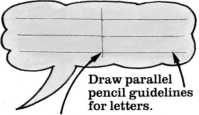

Draw parallel pencil guidelines for letters.

To centre the lettering, draw a vertical line. Then put the same number of words each side (count the spaces between words as one letter).

Use small lettering in a large bubble for quiet speech.

For loud speech, do the opposite.

A line of small circles from the bubble indicates thought.

With more than one speech bubble in a frame, people will read them from the top left corner down to the bottom right corner. Make sure you place them in the order you want them read.

Framing

Use the tips below to vary the size and shape of the picture frames. This makes the strip look more interesting.

Different sized boxes.

Use a circle to highlight a particular moment.

Use a series of zs to show someone or something asleep.

Dinosaur goes over three frames for a before-and-after sequence.

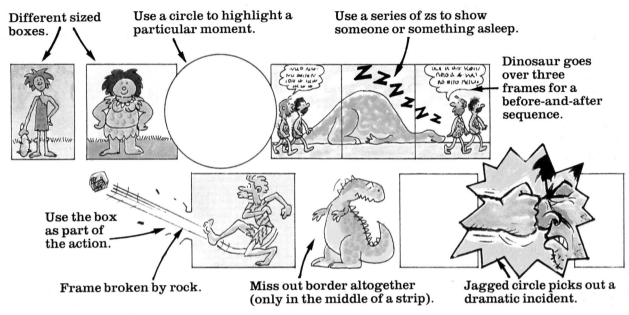

Use the box as part of the action.

Frame broken by rock.

Miss out border altogether (only in the middle of a strip).

Jagged circle picks out a dramatic incident.

A finished strip

This strip cartoon uses some of the techniques described. There are also some more tips for you to follow.

Flash breaking out of frame gives a dramatic effect.

Add extra letters for a long scream.

Hint of smoke leads to next frame.

Movement lines indicate head turning quickly.

Circle broken by elbow.

A close-up varies the look of the pictures.

Different sized frames.

Action continues beyond the last frame.

23

Cartoon lettering

You can make dramatic sound effects for your cartoons. Use colours and shapes that suggest the sound you want to make. Try drawing the words on this page and then use the tips to make up your own words.

The wiggly outlines of the letters make them look as if they have been squashed by the dinosaur's tail.

Draw soft, squelchy letter shapes.

The extra letters give the impression of a long noise. The letters get bigger and bigger to suggest a loud growl.

Drop shadows

You can make the sound have more impact by adding a drop shadow. Use sharp letter angles to suggest a loud sound.

Draw the letter outlines, then trace them on to tracing paper. Use the tracing to draw the shadow under and to the right of the original word.

Black in the shadow. You can also try using coloured letters and shadows.

Extra dimensions

In this example, the word radiates out from the crashing caveman. This helps to give a three-dimensional effect.

Draw the caveman. Mark a point in the centre of his body and draw pencil guidelines radiating out from this point.

Use the guidelines to draw the letters.

Add impact lines last.

24

Moving pictures

For fast-action cartoons there are simple ways to make your characters look as if they are on the run. The two main ways to draw fast running legs are shown in the cartoon below.

Lines around the body suggest movement.

Beads of perspiration.

Leg positions

Horizontal lines add to the speed effect.

Movement lines

Draw feet clear of ground.

The dinosaur's legs are a blurred spiral of lines. The foot shape is repeated again and again around the edge.

The caveman's legs have movement lines to show that he is running. In both methods the feet are clear of the ground.

Movement and distance

Add giant prehistoric ferns. Draw them large in the foreground and smaller as you go into the distance.

Draw figures in the foreground larger than those further away.

Fade the sky colour towards the horizon.

Dust disappears.

Here, dust kicked up by the runners helps to give the impression of movement. Draw the dust clouds smaller as they disappear out of view to give depth to the cartoon.

Ice Age mammals

The earth became very cold in the Ice Ages. Huge sheets of ice spread out from the North and South Poles. Prehistoric mammals in the northern continents had to move south or adapt to the cold. The mammoth, woolly rhinoceros and cave bear had woolly coats to help them survive in the cold.

Woolly rhinoceros

The woolly rhino would have used its large horn to dig up plants.

Colour the whole body with a light brownish ochre wash. Build up the woolly coat by using short brush strokes of dark brown.

Add black brush strokes for extra shadows.

Use dark grey on a pale wash for this wrinkly skin.

Artist's colours

Ochre is a pale brownish yellow.

Cave bear

The prehistoric cave bear was about 4m (13ft) tall on its hind legs – over a third bigger than modern brown bears. Make its coat look furry by building up layers of short brush strokes on a smooth pale layer of background colour.

Colour the bear lightly with a burnt sienna wash. Use darker tones of brown for the fur.

Artist's colours

Burnt sienna is a warm brown.

For a menacing snarl, add teeth with thick white paint against a red mouth.

A crisp, black outline on the claws makes them look sharp.

Mammoth

Mammoths probably used their long tusks to clear snow from plants to eat. Follow the tips below to draw a mammoth in a bleak, wintry scene.

Use cold colours for the sky. Begin with streaks of pale blue and yellow wash. Allow the colours to overlap. Add grey patches for the clouds.

Highlights make the mountains look three dimensional.

Dark shadows on the tusks makes them stand out against the snow.

The snow reflects the sky colours. Use blues and greys for shadows. Add pale pink as well as yellow for highlights.

Colour the mammoth with a burnt sienna wash. Add touches of grey over the brown to give a mottled effect. Then add dark brown mixed with indigo for the shadows.

Cartoon bear

Cartoons are often drawn with just a few, carefully placed lines. The cartoon below is done in this way, which gives it a fresh, lively look.

Caveman's face has no outline. Your eye fills in the missing detail.

Roots drawn as grasping claws add drama.

Fierce and meek animals

When the dinosaurs died out about 65 million years ago, mammals took over the world. Here you can find out how to draw the terrible sabre-toothed tiger, a meek, armoured glyptodon and a fierce meat-eating bird.

Sabre-toothed tiger

This pouncing sabre-toothed cat is a Smilodon (Smile-oh-don). Follow the tips below to make the scene come to life.

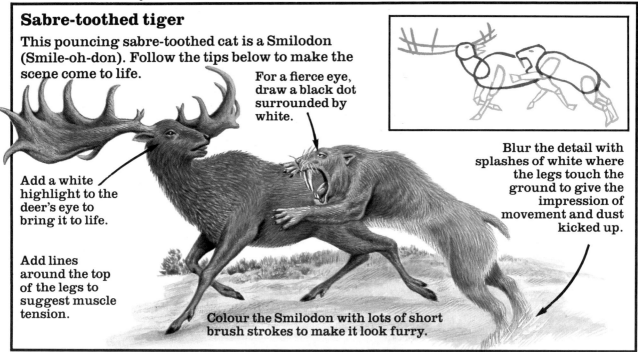

For a fierce eye, draw a black dot surrounded by white.

Add a white highlight to the deer's eye to bring it to life.

Add lines around the top of the legs to suggest muscle tension.

Blur the detail with splashes of white where the legs touch the ground to give the impression of movement and dust kicked up.

Colour the Smilodon with lots of short brush strokes to make it look furry.

Glyptodon

In contrast to the Smilodon, the Glyptodon (Glip-toe-don) was a slow animal that ate insects, worms and berries. Its bony shell and spiky tail helped to protect it against meat eaters. Use lots of highlights on the shell to make it look shiny.

The contrast of highlights and shade helps the shell look rounded.

Add highlights to edges of spots facing the light.

Fine white lines on neck and underside look like fur.

Begin with a dark brown wash. Keep the paint lighter on the side where the light falls. Let it dry before adding the spots.

Use a mixture of white and ochre paint for the spots. Add more ochre to the mix for the shaded areas.

Diatryma

The flightless Diatryma (Die-ah-try-ma) was over three metres tall – nearly as tall as an African elephant. Use the tips on page five to help balance the bird.

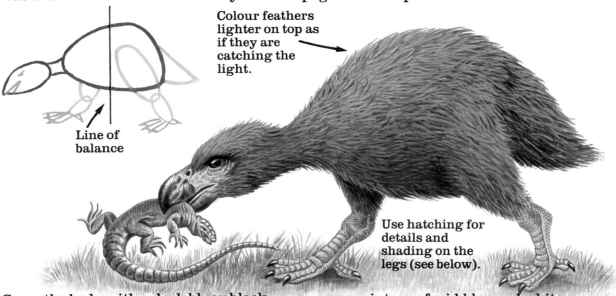

Line of balance

Colour feathers lighter on top as if they are catching the light.

Use hatching for details and shading on the legs (see below).

Cover the body with a dark bluey black wash. When dry, add another layer to the underside for shadow. For the feathers, use a mixture of mid-blue and white. Apply the paint with short flicks of the brush in one direction only.

Cartoon Diatryma

The Diatryma was such a strange looking bird that you only need to simplify its shape slightly to draw this weird cartoon character. Use felt tips for bold colouring.

ANYBODY HOME?

KNOCK KNOCK

29

Dinosaur stencils

You can make a dinosaur stencil from thin card – an empty cereal packet will do. Carefully cut out the animal shape so that you can use both the positive and negative. The simpler the shape, the easier it is to cut out. Use a pair of small, sharp scissors.

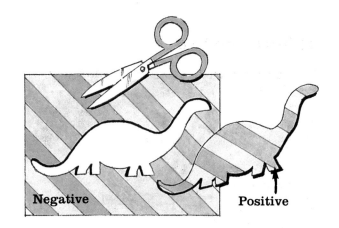

Negative

Positive

Candle wax textures

Candle wax resists paint and leaves interesting patterns. Use thin, white birthday candles. You could copy the diplodocus shape below to make a stencil.

Paint from side to centre.

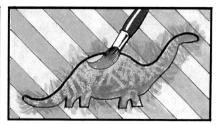

Hold down the negative stencil and cover it with a yellow wash. Use a fairly dry wash or it will seep under the stencil.

When dry, draw wrinkles and scaly patterns over the diplodocus with a candle.

Keep the stencil in place and paint all over the shape with a dark bluey green wash.

Paint plant silhouettes in a pale mauve wash. When dry, draw on stem and leaf shapes in candle wax. Finish with a dark mauve wash on top.

For this sky, paint the sun then cover it with wax. Draw lines and swirls in wax for clouds. Paint over the top with a pink wash fading to yellow.

Apply lines of wax before adding the water colour to look like reflections.

Artist's tip

Cover the dinosaur with the positive stencil when you colour the background. This keeps the dinosaur clean.

Splatter method

This Diplodocus is coloured by flicking paint off a toothbrush.

Lay down the negative stencil and apply a pale green wash. Let this dry.

Then dip a tooth brush into a darker mix of paint. Use your finger or the edge of a ruler to run along the bristles towards you, flicking the paint on to the Diplodocus.

Scratch out eye and mouth shape with a pin.

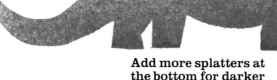

Add more splatters at the bottom for darker shadows.

Chalks and crayons

Reverse the stencil to turn the dinosaur round. This dinosaur is coloured with crayons inside the negative stencil. There is no hard outline and the dinosaur is made to look rounded by the direction of the crayon lines.

Curve the lines around the body.

Build up the body shape with crossing lines.

Add eyes and mouth last with a soft (2B) pencil.

Use chalk on its side to make block shapes in the background.

Artist's tip

Use fixing spray to stop chalks from smudging. You can buy this from most art material shops.

Silhouettes

To make silhouettes, draw outlines first and fill the shapes using black felt tip or ink. Keep background colours light, to make a good contrast with the shapes. You can enlarge the shapes using a grid.*

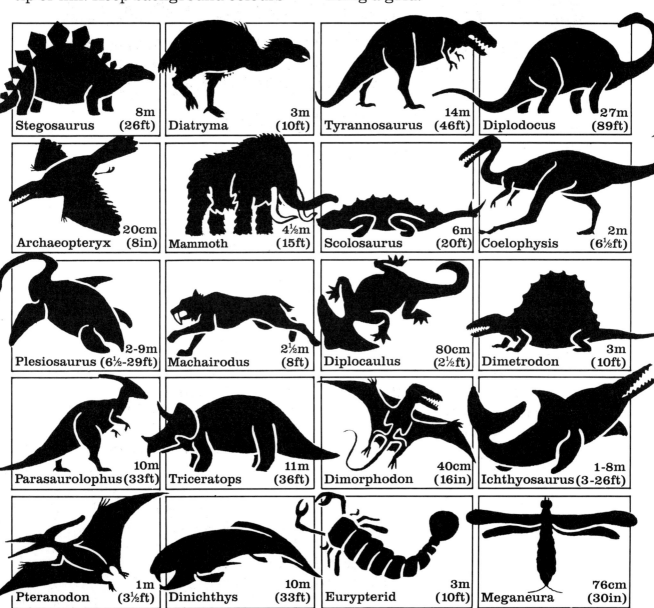

Stegosaurus 8m (26ft)	Diatryma 3m (10ft)
Tyrannosaurus 14m (46ft)	Diplodocus 27m (89ft)
Archaeopteryx 20cm (8in)	Mammoth 4½m (15ft)
Scolosaurus 6m (20ft)	Coelophysis 2m (6½ft)
Plesiosaurus 2-9m (6½-29ft)	Machairodus 2½m (8ft)
Diplocaulus 80cm (2½ft)	Dimetrodon 3m (10ft)
Parasaurolophus 10m (33ft)	Triceratops 11m (36ft)
Dimorphodon 40cm (16in)	Ichthyosaurus 1-8m (3-26ft)
Pteranodon 1m (3½ft)	Dinichthys 10m (33ft)
Eurypterid 3m (10ft)	Meganeura 76cm (30in)

*See how to use grids on page 3.

Part Two
HOW TO DRAW
GHOSTS, VAMPIRES & HAUNTED HOUSES

Emma Fischel

Designed by Kim Blundell

Edited by Janet Cook and Anita Ganeri

**Illustrated by Victor Ambrus, Kim Blundell,
Rob McCaig, Mike Pringle and Graham Round**

Contents

About part two

This part of the book shows you how to draw supernatural things. Some are funny – and some will send shivers down your spine.

Ghosts

On pages 38–45 you can find out how to draw all sorts of different ghosts, for example one that is headless or see-through. Use pages 36–37 to start you off. They show how you can make simple shapes look ghostly by the way you paint them.

These watercolour ghosts are on page 36.

Vampires

Pages 50–53 show you how to draw vampires and all the horrible things associated with them. The picture above of Dracula is on page 53.

Cartoons

There are lots of ideas for funny cartoons in the book, like these cows amazed by the driverless car. On page 51 you can find tips for drawing a cartoon strip.

This cartoon is on page 61.

Haunted houses

You can see how to draw a haunted house on pages 54–55. On pages 56–59 there are all kinds of horrible things you could put inside one, such as the skeleton and spider shown on the left.

Mixing pictures

You could combine different things in the book to make your own ghostly scene. Try drawing a vampire from page 50 creeping through the graveyard on page 48, for example. The haunted house on pages 54–55 would be a good setting for any of the ghosts on pages 38–45. On pages 62–63 there are lots of heads and bodies you could mix to create your own ghost or vampire.

Drawing in stages

Many of the pictures in this book have step-by-step drawing instructions for you to follow. Always copy the outline shapes in pencil. Draw the lines shown in green first, then those shown in red, and lastly the ones shown in blue.

The easiest shapes to draw have one outline.

This raven is on page 48.

This genie is on page 41.

More difficult shapes have two outlines.

Make the outlines the size you want your picture to be.

The hardest shapes to draw have three outlines.

See page 46 for how to draw this ghoul.

Pencils

Pencils are marked with a code which tells you how hard or soft they are. Choose a pencil that suits the kind of drawing you want to do. The different pencils you can use are shown below.

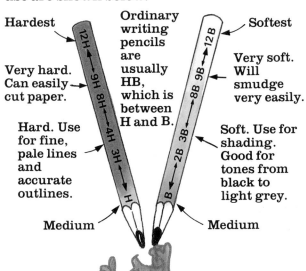

Hardest

Very hard. Can easily cut paper.

Hard. Use for fine, pale lines and accurate outlines.

Ordinary writing pencils are usually HB, which is between H and B.

Medium

Softest

Very soft. Will smudge very easily.

Soft. Use for shading. Good for tones from black to light grey.

Medium

Using a fixative spray

Lots of the pictures in this book are drawn with charcoal, chalks or soft pencils. If you use these you then need to use a fixative spray to stop them smudging.

Hold your drawing upright and spray it from about 40cm away. Use two light coats of spray; one heavy coat will discolour the paper.

This picture is on page 38.

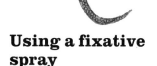

Always use the spray in an open space, preferably outside, as the fumes are dangerous.

Ghostly shapes

What is a ghost? Where do they come from and what do they look like? As no-one really knows, there is no limit to the ways you can draw them. You need to capture the sense of mystery about them because, although people have been telling stories about ghosts for hundreds of years, there is no proof that they even exist.

Here are a few ideas to start you on your way.

Shadowy ghosts

To draw these ghosts you will need to use a soft pencil* and thin rubber. First shade all over a sheet of paper with the pencil, then rub out some of the shading to suggest the ghosts' outlines and faces.

Ghostly background

A good background can help create a ghostly atmosphere. Gloomy castle battlements drawn at an odd angle give this picture an uncomfortable feel.

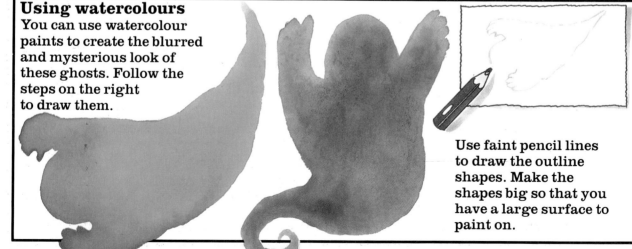

Using watercolours

You can use watercolour paints to create the blurred and mysterious look of these ghosts. Follow the steps on the right to draw them.

Use faint pencil lines to draw the outline shapes. Make the shapes big so that you have a large surface to paint on.

*See page 35 for the different kinds of pencil you can use.

Use pencil to draw first the ghost shape, then the outline of the castle.

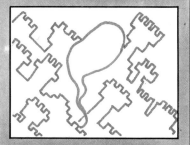

Colour the castle with thick felt tips, using diagonal line strokes to fill in the pencil outline. Colour the ghost with felt tips and add drooping eyes and a mouth.

First paint the shapes with clean water, then paint streaks of watercolours on top. The paints will blend together, making new colours where they mix.

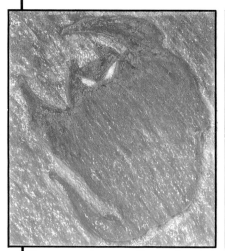

You can use cardboard cut-out shapes to create lots of ghostly effects, like the fiery and devilish ghosts shown above.

To make your cut-out, copy the ghost shape in the pictures above on to a sheet of cardboard and then cut it out with scissors.

Fiery ghost

Put the cut-out on to a smooth surface. Place a sheet of paper over the cut-out.

Rub over the paper with wax crayons, being careful not to move the cut-out.

Colour the top part again, so the ghost appears to fade away at the bottom.

Devilish ghost

Colour a sheet of paper with wax crayons, using lots of different colours.

Cover the whole sheet with a thick layer of black wax crayon.

Create the ghost shape on top by tracing around the cut-out with a dried-up ballpoint pen.

37

Some human ghosts

On these four pages there are lots of human ghosts to draw. Once you have tried them you could use the techniques shown here to make anyone look ghostly. You could turn a pop star or television personality into a see-through ghost, for example, or draw your best friend as a headless ghost . . .

Pirate ghost

There are lots of stories about people who have had violent deaths returning as ghosts. Unable to rest, they are supposed to haunt the scene of their death, like the pirate on the right.

First draw this figure in pencil on a dark sheet of paper. Make it the size you want the finished picture to be.

Draw the lines shown in red. They are the basic shape of the pirate. Rub out the lines shown in green.

Draw the lines shown in blue. Go over all the lines with white chalk, then add the shading.*

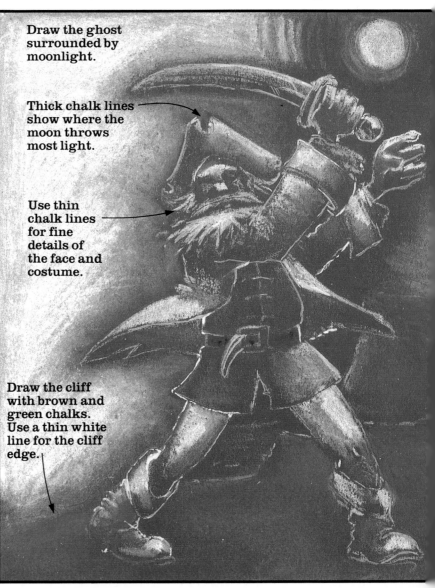

Draw the ghost surrounded by moonlight.

Thick chalk lines show where the moon throws most light.

Use thin chalk lines for fine details of the face and costume.

Draw the cliff with brown and green chalks. Use a thin white line for the cliff edge.

*Use a fixative spray to stop the picture smudging (see page 35).

Drawing a sheet ghost

The idea that ghosts are like figures draped in flowing sheets probably came about because the dead used to be buried in white robes, called shrouds.

You can find an easy way to draw a moving sheet ghost below.

Draw the human shape in pencil. Add a sheet around the shape with a felt tip. Rub out the pencil lines.

Draw thin black lines to show the folds of the sheet. Add a hint of colour with a pencil crayon.

Draw the bottom of the sheet as a point to make the ghost look as if it is floating. Add eyes and a mouth.

As the ghost moves forwards the head gets bigger. The body narrows into a "V" shape at the bottom.

Seeing a ghost

How would you feel if you saw a ghost? Interested or scared? As a cartoon exaggerates normal features and expressions, it is a good way to draw someone looking very frightened by seeing a ghost. Below are three steps to drawing a cartoon face.

Lines round the face and blobs of sweat show he is quaking with fear.

These are called construction lines.

Draw a circle with two pencil lines crossing it.

Eyes equal distances from nose.

Ears level with nose.

Draw the nose where the lines meet. Add the eyes and ears.

Drooping mouth

Rub out the pencil lines and add hair and a mouth.

By making a few changes to the basic cartoon face on the left you can show someone looking really terrified.

Headless ghost

The headless ghost of Anne Boleyn, second wife of Henry VIII of England, is said to haunt Hampton Court in London.   To draw her ghost, first copy the outlines below on to black paper. Make your outline the size you want the finished picture to be.

Use pencil for the outlines.

Rub out the green lines.

Anne Boleyn was beheaded in 1536.

Paint the ghost with white watercolour.* You will need a thick and a thin brush.

Paint the outline and fine details, like the lace, with a thin, wet brush.

Use a thick brush for the folds of material. The brush should be dry and the paint so thick that it will almost not leave the brush.

Put your ghost in a setting such as the doorway shown here.

Doppelganger

This ghost is called a doppelganger. It is the double of a living person.

Paint a face on one half of a sheet of paper. Fold the paper in half. Press the sides together then open them up again.

Use thick, dry paint.

Seeing your doppelganger means you will die soon.

See-through ghosts

A ghost may appear to glide through solid objects. To get a see-through effect you can use watercolours on top of wax. As they don't mix, anything drawn in wax will show through watercolours.

Follow these steps to draw this picture.

1. Draw the background shapes in pencil.

2. Draw the ghosts with thin wax crayons.

Genie

The story of Aladdin and his magic lamp is well known. Every time he rubs the lamp a genie rises out of it in a puff of smoke and grants him a wish.

Use the shapes below to draw the genie.

Draw this outline very big so that you can decorate the costume in some of the ways shown here.

Draw in the details of the face, hands and costume. Add smoke shapes around the outline.

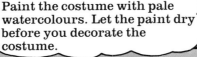

Paint the costume with pale watercolours. Let the paint dry before you decorate the costume.

Cotton reel

Polystyrene

Toothpaste lid

3. Now paint a thin layer of water over the whole picture, then paint streaks of pale watercolours on it while the paper is still wet.

4. Once the paint is dry, go over the pencil lines with thin black felt tip.

Printing

You could make patterns on the costume by dipping any of the things shown above into paint or ink, then pressing them on to the picture.

You could also use potato prints. First cut a potato in half and cut shapes into the flat edge.* Then use the cut edge to make patterns.

*Always cut away from your hand so that you don't cut yourself if the knife slips.

Ghosts from around the world

Every country has its own ghost stories and legends. Here you can see just some of the strange ghosts to be found around the world.

Ghost from Ancient China

In Ancient China, murdered people were said to return as ghosts, appearing from a shapeless cloud and surrounded by green light.

To draw this picture first copy the outlines below. Go over the finished outline with thin green and black ballpoint pens.

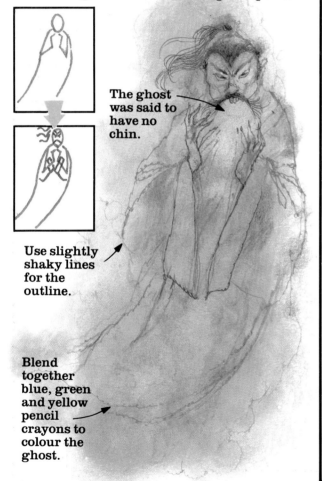

The ghost was said to have no chin.

Use slightly shaky lines for the outline.

Blend together blue, green and yellow pencil crayons to colour the ghost.

Japanese ghost

Use black felt tip to go over the outline.

The Ancient Japanese believed that people who had led evil lives came back as ghosts. As a punishment for their wickedness, their legs were always in flames.

Use the outlines below to help you draw this ghost, then colour it in with felt tips.

Scottish kelpie

This ghost is called a kelpie. You could copy or trace the picture, then colour it with pencil crayons. Use black and purple to draw the outline, and to add details to the face and coat. Use a mixture of colours to shade over the top.

Dark shading shows the muscles.

Use long lines for the tail and mane.

According to Scottish legend, kelpies persuaded unwary travellers to ride them across a river. Once on a kelpie's back, travellers were unable to get off and the kelpie drowned them.

Seeing this dog is supposed to mean certain death.

Phantom hound

This phantom dog, called Barquest, is said to be found near graveyards in France. Use the outline below to draw it, then colour the ghost with black felt tip. Use short, wavy lines to show its shaggy fur.

Egyptian khu

This Ancient Egyptian ghost is called a khu. People believed it caused diseases in human beings and drove animals mad. You can see how to draw it below.

Outline the eyes and beak in black.

First paint a watercolour wash over the paper.* Let it dry, then copy the outlines above in pencil. Draw in the background with fine felt tips and colour the ghost with red felt tip.

See the see-through ghosts on page 40 for how to paint a watercolour wash.

43

Ghostly vehicles

Not all ghosts are of people or animals. A ghostly vehicle may haunt the route of its last journey, replaying the moments of a fatal crash.

Drawing a ghost train

Copy the shape below to draw this ghost train. First draw the green lines to help you get the proportions of the train right. The carriages look smaller as they get further away; this is called perspective.

  Use pastel pencils to colour the train.* Start by using black pastel to define the edges of the train then build up the other colours.

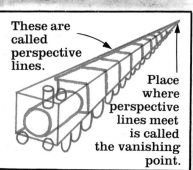

These are called perspective lines.

Place where perspective lines meet is called the vanishing point.

Ghostly fact

In 1879, a Scottish night train plunged off a bridge whose middle section had blown away. It was rebuilt but years later a silent train was seen rushing over it, vanishing where the bridge had collapsed.

Add steam with white pastel.

Smooth in colour by rubbing it with a soft rag.

Yellow and white shading shows where lightning highlights part of the train.

White lines give impression of speed.

Draw rails with black and purple line strokes.

44   *Prevent smudging with a fixative spray (see page 35).*

The carriages eventually look so small that they disappear. This happens at the vanishing point.

Things in the distance appear fainter and more blurred than they do close up.

Phantom ship

To draw this ship, first dampen a sheet of paper with water. Dab runny poster or powder paints on to the sheet with a brush. The colours will spread on the wet paper.

Once the paint is dry, draw the ship with grey felt tip. Add foam by dabbing thick white paint round the ship with a rag or tissue.

This is the ghost of The Palatine. It was looted and set on fire in 1752. Each anniversary its blazing ghost is said to sail along the North American coast.

Drawing your own ghostly vehicle

Now try creating your own ghostly lorry, based on the outline on the right. First, follow the grid method shown below to make the lorry the size you want your finished picture to be.

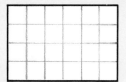

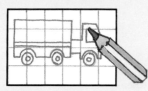

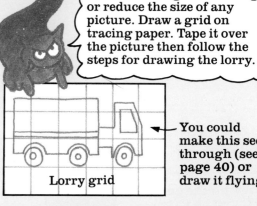

You can use a grid to enlarge or reduce the size of any picture. Draw a grid on tracing paper. Tape it over the picture then follow the steps for drawing the lorry.

Lorry grid

You could make this see-through (see page 40) or draw it flying.

Draw a grid with the same number of squares as the lorry grid. The size of your lorry will depend on how big the squares are.

Look at the shape in each square of the lorry grid. Copy it on to the same square in your grid. Rub out the grid lines.

You can adapt the grid method to draw any vehicle you like. How about a phantom tractor, ocean-going liner, car, rocket, or even a UFO?

Ghost train ride

A ride on a ghost train can be a terrifying experience. Once the train moves into the tunnel there is only one way out: forward . . .

On these pages you can see how to draw just some of the ghastly things that might be lurking round the next bend in the track.

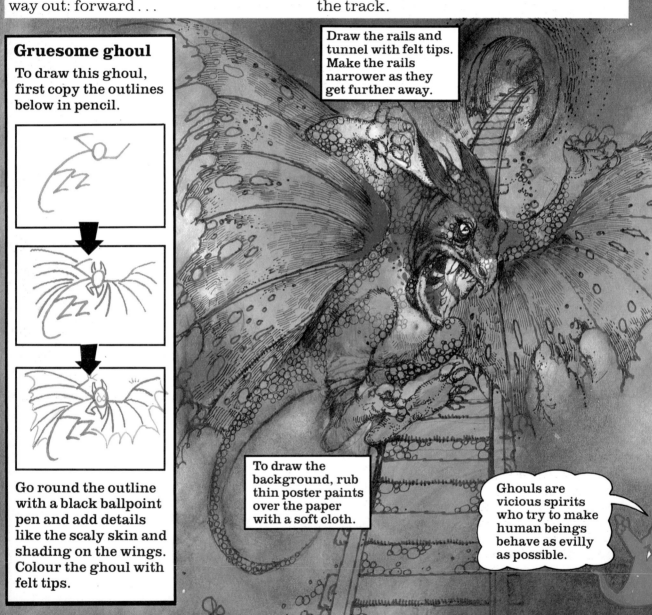

Gruesome ghoul

To draw this ghoul, first copy the outlines below in pencil.

Go round the outline with a black ballpoint pen and add details like the scaly skin and shading on the wings. Colour the ghoul with felt tips.

Draw the rails and tunnel with felt tips. Make the rails narrower as they get further away.

To draw the background, rub thin poster paints over the paper with a soft cloth.

Ghouls are vicious spirits who try to make human beings behave as evilly as possible.

Grinning skull

To draw this skull, first copy or trace the picture. Go round the outline in black and colour it in with felt tips.

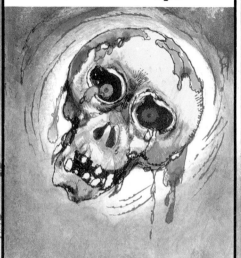

Colour the yellow areas, then add green and orange on top. Use bright colours for the slime and eyes. Fill in the black areas and add fine details with red and black ballpoint pens.

Ghostly fiend

This hideous fiend is drawn using watercolours, ballpoint pens and pencil crayons.

First paint a thin layer of pale green watercolour over the page. Once the paint is dry, copy the outline shapes below on to the paint using faint pencil lines.

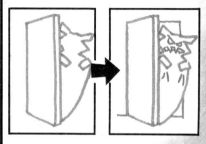

Copy details of the face and doorway from the main picture, using black, green and red ballpoint pens. Shade the doorway and the fiend's clothes with green and black pencil crayons.

Cobwebs

To draw a cobweb on the wall of your tunnel, first copy the outline on the right. Draw over it with a black ballpoint pen, using shaky line strokes to suggest that the web is quite fragile.

Add a black spider crawling out from the middle of its web.

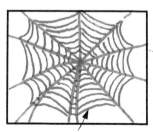

Continue drawing the lines shown in red until your cobweb is the size you want.

Graveyards

Graveyards are quiet and mysterious places, full of strange shapes and dark trees, with a history that may go back hundreds of years.

These pages show you how to draw a graveyard and the things you might expect to find in it – as well as some you might hope not to.

Drawing the graveyard

The shapes of things in the graveyard are quite simple to draw. It is the way they are coloured that creates the atmosphere.

This picture was coloured with pencil crayons. On the opposite page you will find lots of tips on shading with crayons to get different effects.

Rub out a curved shape, then draw in the bats.

Draw pale, slanting lines to give the graveyard a misty look.

The raven is said to be a herald of death.

This is the Graveyard Guardian, the spirit of the first person buried in the graveyard. It returns to protect the other graves from evil.

To give the stone a textured look, put sandpaper under the page when you colour the tomb.

Raven

Use the outline above to help you draw this raven. Colour it with black pencil crayon, using short line strokes to show its ragged feathers. Use darker shading under the body to show its rounded shape.

Draw shadows with purple and black crayons.

Use blue and green pencil crayons to draw in yew trees, which are always found in graveyards.

Use this outline to help you draw the church.

Stained glass window

Follow the stages below to draw the stained glass windows on the church.

First, draw the arch shape in pencil and a line of the pattern down the middle of the window. Next, build up the shapes on either side.

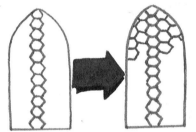

Go over the outlines with a thin black pen and colour the shapes with felt tips.

Add extra lines to simple shapes.

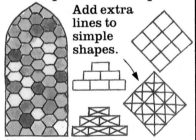

Above you can also see suggestions for different patterns you could use.

Graveyard Guardian

To draw the Graveyard Guardian, start with the outlines on the right. Colour it in with pencil crayons, using blue and grey for the folds of the robe and darker colours inside the hood.

A Graveyard Guardian has no face.

Technique tips

Below you can see the different shading methods used in the main picture.*

Hatching

Cross-hatching

Stippling

Texturing

Smudging

Rubbing out

*See page 35 for the different kinds of pencil you can use.

49

Vampires

Vampires are said to be living corpses who feed on human blood. They leave the grave at sunset in search of human victims. These pages show some of the strange ways a vampire might behave. There could be many more . . .

Drawing a cartoon vampire

To draw this cartoon vampire, first copy the figures below.

Draw deadly fangs for piercing victims' necks.

Add a shadow.

Copy the figure shown in green to get the proportions of the body right. Draw the cloak around the body and add details to the face. Colour the vampire with felt tips.

Moving vampires

Use the green figures to help you draw these moving vampires. Fill in the body shapes around the figures.

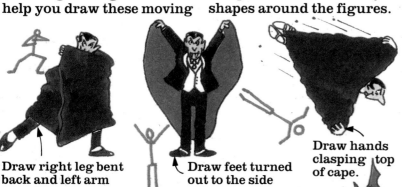

Draw right leg bent back and left arm round face.

Draw feet turned out to the side

Draw hands clasping top of cape.

Vampire victim

A vampire hypnotizes its victims so that they do not struggle and will remember nothing of the attack.

Use the outlines below to help you draw this vampire victim. As she is looking to one side, the position of her features is different from the cartoon face on **page 39**.

Vertical construction line is curved.

Line across stays the same.

Eyes move round.

Ears move so only one shows.

Nose moves to where lines meet.

Vampires return night after night until their victims die. Then they too become vampires.

50

Vampire cartoon strip

Artists use lots of ways to make cartoon strips look interesting and funny. Below are some professional tips which you could use to create your own vampire cartoon strip.

Short piece of text sets time and place.

Jagged edge to speech bubble suggests a ringing sound.

Shape of letters can help to emphasize the word.

Put bubbles over uncluttered areas.

It is mainly the pictures that tell the story, not the text.

A vampire has no reflection in a mirror.

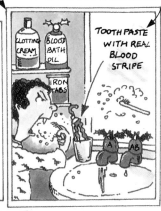

Use unusual viewpoints.

Conversation starts here as people read from left to right.

Vary close-ups and longer views.

Different size frames add interest.

Strip should end with a strong punch-line.

Other vampire characters

Here are some suggestions for other characters you could use in your vampire cartoon strip.

Baby Vamp

Fang the spider

Granny Vamp and Tibbles

Drawing a werewolf

Werewolves are human beings who change into savage, wolf-like creatures when there is a full moon. They live on human flesh and can only be killed by a silver bullet or knife. They have to be burnt when they die. If they are buried they become vampires.

To draw this werewolf, first copy these outlines.

Use thin black felt tip to draw his hair. Outline his features, then draw wrinkled skin using short felt tip line strokes. Colour the whole picture with pencil crayons.

Vampire hands

Vampire hands are very thin and bony. Hands are difficult to draw, so use the steps below to help you.

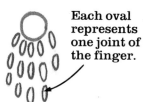

Each oval represents one joint of the finger.

Draw green veins.

Rub out the ovals before adding details.

First, draw the hand as a series of oval shapes.

Next, draw the hand outline round the ovals.

Add details like the nails and knuckles.

More hands to draw

Here are some suggestions for drawing vampire hands in other positions.

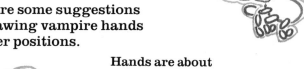

Hands are about as long as the distance from a person's chin to their hairline.

Bats

Vampires can turn themselves into bats to fly through windows and attack their sleeping victims.

These bats are drawn with black and red felt tips. Use the outlines to help you draw them.

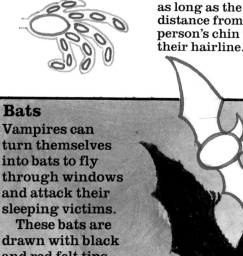

Add eyes and a mouth.

Dracula

The most famous vampire of all is the evil Count Dracula. He first appeared as a character in a book by Bram Stoker in 1897.

Here Dracula is about to carry out one of his ghastly attacks. Try tracing this picture, then use the tips below to colour it.

Use this outline to help you draw the part of the cloak hidden by the parchment.

1. Colour the outside of his cloak, his hair and bow tie with black poster paint. Use red on the inside of his cloak and top of his waistcoat, then add the red details to his mouth and round his eyes. Paint his trousers grey. Let this dry, then add black stripes.

2. Colour his skin and waistcoat with pencil crayons.

3. Use short, fine lines of green and black ballpoint pen to add further shading to his clothes and skin, then draw the pattern round the top of his waistcoat.

Story of Dracula

In Bram Stoker's story, Dracula lived in a huge rambling castle in Transylvania in eastern Europe. He wanted to fill the world with vampires and planned to start in England. He travelled there by ship, killing all the crew and drinking their blood. He terrorized London with a wave of vampire attacks but was chased back to Transylvania and killed by a knife being stabbed through his heart.

Haunted houses

Everyone knows what makes a house look haunted – or do they? How do you draw echoing footsteps, strange noises or sudden icy draughts?

Here are some ideas for ways to create a menacing atmosphere and suggest an unseen ghostly presence.

Drawing the picture

To draw the picture on the right, first paint the sky across the whole page. You can see how to draw it and the rest of the background on the opposite page. Once the sky is dry draw the house on top, using the shapes below to help. Paint the house following the tips below, then add the trees and other details.

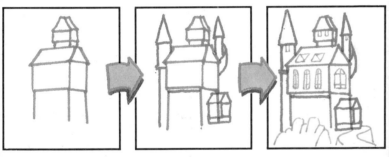

Painting the house

The picture is painted in gouache, a form of watercolour professional artists often use. Its advantage over ordinary watercolours is that light colours can be painted on top of dark ones. If you don't have gouache, you could use poster paints.

The house casts lots of strange and sinister shadows. To paint them, first copy the dark areas on the left in pencil.

Now fill them in with black poster paint. Let the paint dry then paint the rest of the shape mid-grey. You can see how to add more detail on the opposite page.

Adding detail

The main types of brickwork are shown on the right. Use quite thick poster paint for them, so that they show up well. Make sure the original layer of grey paint is dry before you start.

White oblongs

Grey oblongs

White lines

Grey lines

Copy the picture for more detailed shading, like that on the windows. Use pale blue to highlight parts of the house not in direct moonlight. Draw trailing plants with strokes of green paint, and add a light in the window with yellow paint.

Drawing the background

The background plays a large part in creating the ghostly effect of this picture. Below are some tips to help you draw it.

Use wavy lines of brown paint for the tree. Let it dry and add white highlights. Draw the flying leaves with blobs of brown and yellow paint.

▶

◀ Paint the sky dark blue. Add other shades on top, letting each colour dry before you add the next. Draw the rain with white chalk lines once the picture is completed.

You can see how to draw bats on page 52.

Inside the house

The rooms inside a haunted house may have been kept locked for hundreds of years, left exactly as they were after some terrible tragedy.

Here, the outer wall has been cut away to show the inside of the haunted house. Use ideas from this picture to create your own haunted room. On the next two pages you can see how to draw some of the strange things in this picture.

A cat senses a strange atmosphere and hisses for no apparent reason.

Light from the moon reveals a trapdoor in the floor.

A grandfather clock chiming thirteen means there will soon be a death in the family.

Years of neglect have caused cracks and cobwebs.

Bloodstains cannot be removed, no matter how much they are scrubbed.

Drawing in the floorboard lines gives a three-dimensional feel to the picture.

Adding interest

A haunted room will look more interesting if you draw the main objects in unusual positions or at unexpected angles. Put objects of different shapes and heights near each other to add variety.

Decide where the light is coming from before you start to draw. Then you can use it to create a ghostly atmosphere, by drawing lots of shadows, for example.

Poltergeists

Poltergeists are invisible spirits who cause chaos in a house by seeming to give objects a life of their own.

You cannot see poltergeists but you can certainly see their effects. Furniture flies across a room and smashes to pieces, objects appear from nowhere, mirrors break or musical instruments start to play by themselves.

Ghostly breezes make the curtains sway, although there is no draught in the room.

The skeleton of a forgotten prisoner is slumped in the corner of a torture chamber.

You can see how to draw this skeleton on the next page.

Poltergeist is a German word. It means noisy spirit.

A secret room is used to hide from enemies. It is reached by stairs hidden behind the fake fireplace.

Moving the front of the fake fireplace reveals a secret door.

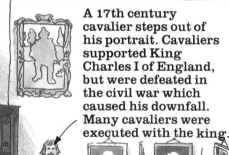

A 17th century cavalier steps out of his portrait. Cavaliers supported King Charles I of England, but were defeated in the civil war which caused his downfall. Many cavaliers were executed with the king.

Echoing footsteps can be heard and ghostly prints appear as if from nowhere.

Ghostly fact

An ancient story tells of a woman who wanted her skull built into a wall of her house when she died, but, despite her wishes, she was buried in the family vault. Immediately afterwards, loud crashing noises, groans and slamming doors were heard. The family decided to do what she asked. The skull was built into a wall and there was peace again.

Skeleton

To draw this skeleton, first copy the outlines shown below it. Draw round the finished outline with black felt tip. Colour the bones with a mixture of pale blue and grey watercolours.

An adult skeleton has 206 bones. These are the main ones.

The ribs gradually get narrower.

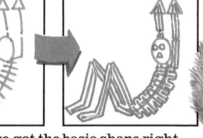

Once you have got the basic shape right, you could try drawing your skeleton in different poses, like the three below.

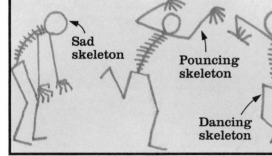

Sad skeleton

Pouncing skeleton

Dancing skeleton

Cats and rats...

You could draw the cat below hissing at an empty chair, or the rat gnawing on a piece of mouldy food.

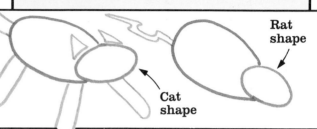

Rat shape

Cat shape

Drawing fur

To draw fur, first paint a thin wash of watercolour over the body. When it is dry, draw lots of short pencil crayon lines over the top.

Draw sharp front teeth and evil red eyes.

Add a shadow under the body.

Draw the ears bent right back.

Draw the whiskers sticking straight out.

Leave the paws white.

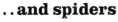

...and spiders

To draw this spider, first pencil in a circle for the head and a larger oval shape for the body. Add eight legs and colour the spider with pencil crayons.

Short lines round the outline make it look hairy.

Portrait ghost

You could copy or trace this portrait ghost or, if you want to make your picture bigger than this, use a grid.* Colour the ghost with a mixture of watercolours and pencil crayons.

Use fine shading lines on his face.

Paint the picture frame yellow, then add patterns with pencil crayons.

Grandfather clock

Draw the basic shapes of this clock in pencil. Colour with pencil crayons to suggest the texture and patterns in the wood, using shades of light and dark brown.

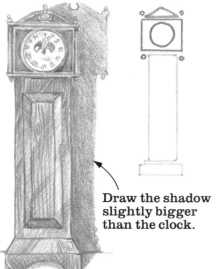

Draw the shadow slightly bigger than the clock.

Texture

Use three shades of watercolour to paint the ghost's jacket and trousers.

First paint a thin wash with the lightest shade.

Let it dry, then paint the middle shade on top, leaving some parts pale.

Use the dark shade to paint areas of shadow.

Pale areas suggest the soft material.

Paint the boots with pale brown watercolour. Let it dry, then shade with a dark pencil crayon.

*See page 45 for how to use a grid.

Drawing the unexpected

One way of suggesting that a ghost may be present is by drawing ordinary objects doing something completely unexpected. These pages show you how to draw things that could never possibly happen — or could they?

Floating table

To draw a picture of a floating table, you need to put it on a background which shows that the table is up in the air.

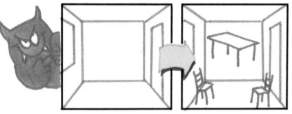

First draw the floor and walls, then the door and window. Make your picture large to leave room for the furniture.

Draw the table and chairs and rub out the background lines behind them. Add details from the main picture.

Colour the picture with pencil crayons. →

Add shadows underneath the furniture.

Ghostly shadows

You can get really funny effects by giving a shadow its own identity, separate from the person or object it belongs to. Try copying the ones below, then think up some shadow pictures of your own. You could make a shadow dance or draw a spiky plant shadow, for example.

Draw in the floor line. ↘

Use solid blocks of colour to fill in the shadows.

Draw a mantlepiece under the clock.

This shadow has become a ghostly monster.

Vanishing kettle

To draw these pictures of a kettle gradually being swallowed up by its own steam, first copy the three kettle shapes in pencil. Sketch in the steam, making it bigger at each stage.

Use charcoal to fill in the outlines, smudging it with your finger to get the rounded shapes of the kettle and steam.* Add eyes and a gaping mouth to the steam.

Areas left white give the kettle a metallic shine.

Crazy cartoons

The piano and car in these cartoons seem to have a life of their own – or is some strange invisible presence at work? Use the shapes below to help you draw them.

Now add detail to the outline shapes, using the finished pictures as guides. Colour your pictures with felt tips, using darker shades to outline the shapes and paler ones inside.

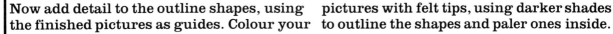

*Use a fixative spray to stop the picture smudging (see page 35).

Mix and match

Here are lots of suggestions for different parts of ghost and vampire bodies. You can mix them in any combination for really peculiar results.

Try drawing a tiptoeing vampire with a chuckling ghost's head or an angry ghost with knocking knees, for example.

Sheet ghosts

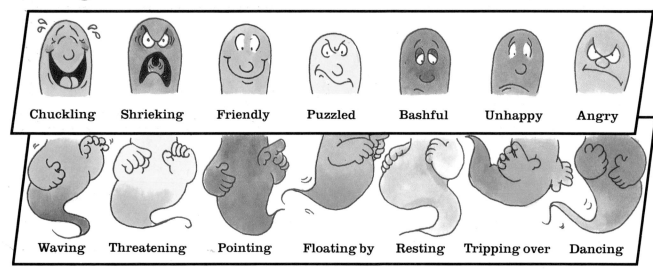

Chuckling	Shrieking	Friendly	Puzzled	Bashful	Unhappy	Angry

Waving	Threatening	Pointing	Floating by	Resting	Tripping over	Dancing

Vampires

Sly	Thirsty	Gleeful	Angry	Tired	Thoughtful	Shifty

Tiptoeing	Creeping	Climbing	Jumping	Crawling	Swooping	Lurking

Seeing ghosts

Shocked — Anxious — Puzzled — Alarmed — Sickly — Petrified — Disappearing fast

Wringing hands — Fingers crossed — Pointing — Walking — Tripping over — Running — Quick getaway

Standing — Climbing — Knees knocking — Walking — Tripping over — Running — Help!

Things to add

Sinister butler — Batty clock — Bone china — Night watchman — Bone chair — Talking heads — Deadly duo — Creepy crawly — Bat walking stick

Ghostly silhouettes

Silhouettes can give your drawings an extra creepy feel. Draw outlines of the figures in pencil. Fill in the shapes using black felt tip or ink.

Bone head

Frankenstein

Creepy cobweb

Terror train

Freaky tree

Angry owl

Grisly graves

Vampire

Spooky spider

Creepy castle

Skeleton

Vampire bats

Sheet ghost

Werewolf

Wicked witch

Hissing cat

Genie

Pumpkin face

Headless ghost

Ghastly ghoul

Part Three
HOW TO DRAW
LETTERING

Judy Tatchell and Carol Varley

Consultant: Graham Peet

Designed by
Nigel Reece and Richard Johnson

Illustrated by Fiona Brown and Guy Smith

Hand lettering by David Young

Additional illustrations by
Chris Smedley and Robin Lawrie

Contents

About lettering

Look around you and you see lettering everywhere. As well as in magazines, books and newspapers, it appears on shop signs, clothes, food wrappers and so on.

This part shows you how to design and do your own lettering. Below are some tips on how to choose a style that will suit your message.

Making a message clear

The most important thing about lettering is that it makes its message clear.

If a message is long or complicated you will need to use a simple style that is easy to read. Fancy styles are harder to read so they should be kept for short messages or greetings.

Books for young children need simple lettering that is easy to recognize.

It is harder to read this fancy lettering.

Choosing a style

A short message looks exciting and comes across well if you pick a lettering style that suits the message. Sometimes, the way the letters look can say almost as much as the words they form.

You can make letters look graceful...

...hurried...

...or technical.

You can combine letters with pictures.

Large or small?

Using very large or very small letters is a bit like talking loudly or softly. Messages that have to stand out and be noticed by passers-by need large, bold letters. This is like saying them in a loud, clear voice.

A poster has to grab people's attention – like a loud announcement.

Small lettering is more like normal conversation.

Using lettering

You can use lettering on cards, letters, projects, posters, T-shirts or just notes to friends. Later in the book, you can find out how to make several copies of your lettering using simple printing methods.

Notes

T-shirts

Labels

Cards

Tools and materials

Throughout the book there is information about paper, pens and materials you can use for lettering.

You can do most of the styles in this book with just colour pencils, felt-tip pens and watercolour paints.

Copying letters

You may like to copy some of the lettering you see in this book. These tips will help you draw the letters accurately. You need a sharp pencil.

The lines are called guidelines.

First draw some lines to help keep the lettering straight.

Keep your wrist still.

Sketch the outline of each letter. Let your wrist rest on the page and move only your fingers.

Use light strokes to sketch the letter.

Move your hand to a convenient position to draw each part of the letter.

Try to keep the outline smooth.

Go over the outline with a fine pen. You can leave it as it is or fill it in.

Lettering techniques

The following techniques help you to keep your letters the same size and in a straight line. You can use them with all kinds of lettering. They will help you to make the styles in this book look smart and professional.

Keeping letters even

You can keep your letters level and even by drawing faint pencil rules, called guidelines.

Unless you want very thin or very fat-looking letters, the distance between the guidelines should be between three and nine times the thickest part of your letter.

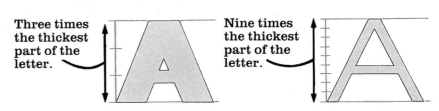

Three times the thickest part of the letter.

Nine times the thickest part of the letter.

Guidelines too far apart for the thickness of the letter: letter looks very thin.

Guidelines too close for the thickness of the letter: letter looks very fat.

Moving the middle

You can also draw a guideline to position the strokes across the middles of some letters. Moving this guideline up or down changes the look of the letters, as shown.

About pencils

Pencils are described by how hard or soft their leads are. The usual range is from 7B (softest) to 6H (hardest). A medium pencil is called HB. A 2B, an HB and a 2H are enough to start with.

A hard pencil makes a thin, greyish line. A soft pencil makes a thicker, blacker line which is easily smudged.

Hard pencils are useful for drawing faint guidelines. A softer pencil is probably better for sketching letter shapes.

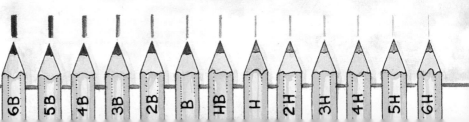

6B 5B 4B 3B 2B B HB H 2H 3H 4H 5H 6H

Small letters

Small letters are just over half as tall as capitals. Small letter sticks (ascenders) and tails (descenders) extend above and below the guidelines by about the same amount. You can vary this for different effects, though.

Ascender

Capital letters also come up to this line.

Descender

Small letter guidelines.

Flowing letters

You can use an italic nib (see below) to do this flowing, joined-up style.

Try using just one guideline through the middle of the letters. It keeps them level but not absolutely even, so they look less rigid.

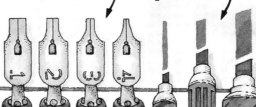

Try a single, curved guideline.

Spacing tips

Leave a space the size of a capital "E" between words made up of capital letters.

RRY E CHR

Leave the space of a small "n" between words made up of small letters.

ceruponnanti

About italic pens

For some of the styles in this book, you need a square-nibbed, or italic, pen. This gives a variety of thick and thin lines. You can find out more about italic writing on page 86.

You can put different italic nibs on a dip pen and use them with a bottle of ink.

You can buy felt pens with broad, flat italic-shaped ends from art shops.

To test whether you are holding the pen nib at the right angle, draw a cross. Both strokes should be the same thickness.

Hold the nib at this angle.

Atmospheric lettering

Some letters set a scene or create an atmosphere by their shape or the way they are decorated.

Decorating letters

The o, f, t and m on the right have all had their shapes adapted to help create an atmosphere. The s and the c have just been decorated. Colour also helps to give atmosphere.

Decorating letters is called illumination. You can find out more on page 84.

Ancient letters

These letters look old and battered. You can get this effect by enlarging typed letters lots of times on a photocopier. A typewriter with a fabric ribbon produces the best results.

The letters break up as tiny faults get bigger and bigger. The more you photocopy them, the more aged the letters look.

Metallic letters

Metallic letters look hard and stylish. Here, the position of the sparkle and highlights makes it look as if light is shining on the letter from the top left.

Hot. Red, orange and yellow are warm colours.

Cold. Icy blues and greens are cold colours.

Natural. The letter looks as if it is alive and growing.

Festive.

Marine. The outline ripples, like water.

Horrific.

These letters have been photocopied 20 times and enlarged 100% each time.

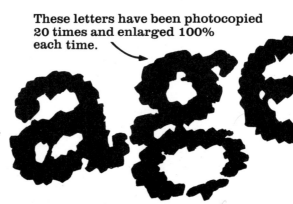

Sparkle
Highlight
Keep this area pale.
Bands of reflected colour.

Add the sparkle by flicking a sharp pencil away from the letter. Make two flicks join at a point.

Secret messages

A quick way to do lettering without doing it by hand is to use newspaper and magazine print. Here, different styles have been torn out roughly. This is supposed to resemble an anonymous message such as a kidnap ransom note.

You could use this sort of style for a joke. No one would expect a Valentine's Day message to be written in such a threatening style.

You can use whole words or make them up out of separate letters. Vary the size and style of the letters.

Digital style

This style makes a message look as if it might have come from a computer.

You could punch holes down the sides to make it look like computer print-out.

Most of the letters are made up from the same set of straight lines.

You have to make a few adjustments to prevent O looking like D, for example, or to complete Q.

Making an envelope

Put your card in the middle of a square of paper. There should be some space between the corners of the card and the paper's edges.

The paper needs to be strong but you must be able to fold it easily.

Fold each corner in round the card, one at a time.

Remove the card. Cut the triangles out where the folds cross (marked red).

Fold the bottom up and glue the sides to it.

Put your card inside. You can glue the top down or stick a cut-out shape over the join.

Time travel

You can give your letters a historical feel by copying the different styles people have used through the ages.

Gothic script

This style is based on a centuries-old script called gothic. Before printing was invented, books were copied out, usually by monks. They wrote in a style like the one below.

Gothic style has often been used for horror film and story titles. Above are some ideas for using a ghoulish gothic style.

You need a broad italic pen for this style. If you don't have one, try drawing the outlines of the letters and colouring them in. (There is a gothic alphabet to copy or adapt on page 94.)

The letters are squarish and angular. Small letters are made up of straight lines.

Capital letters are highly decorated.

Sampler lettering

An embroidered design made up of letters, numbers, pictures and words is called a sampler. This one was sewn by an 11 year old girl in 1760.

You can do letters which look as if they are made up of tiny stitches. Keep your crayons sharp or the "stitch" thickness will vary.

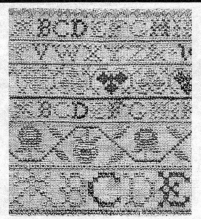

It is easiest to work on squared paper. Draw a letter outline in pencil, made up of straight lines. Fill it in with tiny crosses. Then rub out the outline.

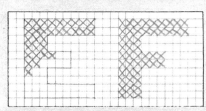

Art Nouveau

In the late 19th century, an artistic style called Art Nouveau developed. Art Nouveau lettering looks good when it is designed decoratively into a picture.

The letters below are natural shapes, like the trees. There is an Art Nouveau-style alphabet for you to copy or adapt on page 95.

page 95.

Letters are designed into the picture and form part of it, rather than being added on top.

The letter shapes reflect the shape of the trees in the pictures.

1930s style

1930s design was elegant and precise. The shapes needed no decoration.

ABC 123

For capital letters in this 30s style, draw a simple letter shape. Thicken one side with downstrokes.

abcdefghi

Small letters have a round shape and a uniform thickness.

This style is good for short messages which need to be clear but stylish.

Here are some different stitch styles for you to try, and some ideas for pictures to go with them.

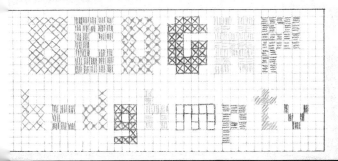

More lettering techniques

Here are some techniques that can make your lettering look very dramatic. They work particularly well with big, capital letters.

Letters in perspective

Horizon

Space dots out evenly on a vertical line.

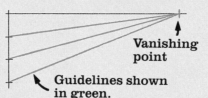

Vanishing point

Guidelines shown in green.

The upright lines remain vertical.

Do the letters closer together as they get further away.

Finally, rub out the guidelines.

Using a fairly hard pencil, such as a 2H, mark three dots on a vertical line. Then draw a horizon line further up the page.

Mark a point on the horizon. This is called the vanishing point. Join each dot to it. Use the lines as your guidelines.

Shadow lettering

Vanishing point

The top of the shadow will fall on this line.

Draw the outline of a letter, a horizon and a vanishing point. Add a line where you want the top of the shadow to fall.

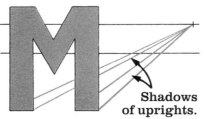

Shadows of uprights.

Draw lines from the uprights to the vanishing point. These lines show you where to position the shadows of the uprights.

Rub out the guidelines.

Use your judgement to position the other lines. Experiment until they look right.

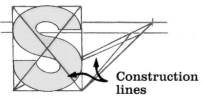

Construction lines

Curved letters are not easy. You can draw some extra lines, called construction lines, to help you.

For the shadow, follow how the upright letter fits into its construction lines.

Letters in a word all go to the same vanishing point. You can rub out the letters and just keep the shadows.

Solid letters

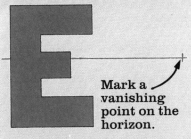

Mark a vanishing point on the horizon.

To make a letter look solid, first draw the letter outline. Then do a horizon just over half way up the letter.

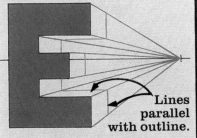

Lines parallel with outline.

Draw lines from the corners of the letter to the vanishing point. Then draw lines parallel with the letter's outline.

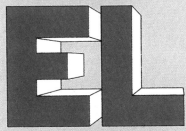

Rub out the guidelines for one letter before starting another. Colour the faces and bodies of the letter.

A word tower

This word tower is coloured like worn stone to make it look monumental. The steps below show you how to construct one like it.

High vanishing point.

Guidelines showing letter heights.

Vanishing point on base line.

Construction lines

Darker colour for chips.

1. Draw a base line showing the width of the lowest letter. Mark a vanishing point in the middle of it. Mark another vanishing point high up, directly above it.

2. Draw guidelines from either end of this base line to the top vanishing point.

3. Draw guidelines to show the height of each letter. Letters get shorter as they get higher up. Then draw in the fronts of the letters.

4. To make the letters look solid, first draw lines from the corners and edges to the lower vanishing point.

5. Shade in the undersides of the letters. Do a letter at a time, ink in a chipped outline and rub out the construction lines. Colour a rough surface.

COMIC STRIP LETTERING

Looking at a comic strip is like a mix between watching a film and reading a story. A comic strip story is told partly in pictures and partly in words.

The lettering must be easy to read but it has several jobs to do. It shows what people say or think in bubbles. It contributes to the sense of drama and also provides sound effects.

The comic strip on these two pages contains examples of lettering used in all these ways.

Comic strip titles

A title must stand out and suit the story. These styles and titles have been mixed up. Can you match the styles to the titles?*

Picture frames

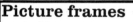

Round   Oblong   No frame

 Picture breaks out.

Jagged

Square

Boxes round the pictures are called frames. Varying frame style keeps the strip lively. You can find all the frame styles above in the strip on the right.

You can draw the frames freehand. This gives your strip a relaxed look.

*Answer: Dream Boy should be in the style of Space Station Alpha. Space Station Alpha should be in the style of Gas Street Gang. Gas Street Gang should be in the style of Dream Boy.

Sound effects

A sound effect is a kind of picture of a sound. There are several in the strip below. Here are some more to inspire you.

Speech bubbles

A speech bubble can show how words are said. For instance, small letters in a big bubble make words look quiet.

Centring letters

Speech bubbles look neat if you centre the letters. See below for how to do this.

Count the letters and spaces on each line:

Count fat letters such as w and m as three units.

Medium letters such as h, n and o are two units.

Spaces and thin letters such as i and t are one unit.

A capital letter has one extra unit.

Draw a vertical line. Put an equal number of units either side of it.

Use a thin black pen for the letters. Then draw a bubble outline around them.

People read from left to right, top to bottom. Position speech bubbles in the frame so that they will be read in the right order.

MAKING POSTERS

The most important thing about lettering on a poster is that it catches people's attention and is easy to read from a distance.

Materials

The size of the paper you use for a poster depends on how far away you want the poster to be seen from.

Poster for a notice-board.	A poster to go outside needs to be much bigger.

The lettering on a poster needs space around it. This will help the message to stand out. Make sure that the paper you choose is big enough for this.

Poster paper comes in different colours.

You can buy different kinds of paper from art shops. If your poster is going outside where it might get wet, buy a harder, less absorbent type of paper.

Use poster paint or gouache that does not run in the wet.

Designing a poster

First, write down what you want to say. Keep it simple.

1- (Birthday party) on
3 (Friday) at (6·00) 4
at (Emma's house) 2

Then divide the message up and number the parts in order of importance. You need to make the most important words stand out.

Finally, choose a suitable style for the message and any illustration.

See opposite page for how to distort letters like this.

Drop shadows

To do a drop shadow, draw a letter. Then copy the outline a bit to the side, and above or below the letter shape. Fill in the shadow a darker shade.

Making letters bigger

If you want to copy small letters on to your poster, you can enlarge them to the right size using a grid.*

Draw a grid on tracing paper. Use about four squares to the height of the letter. Place it over the letter you want to copy.

Draw a larger grid on the poster the size you want the letter to be. Use a faint pencil line so you can rub the grid out later.

Copy what appears in each square of the small grid into the larger grid.

Squash and stretch

You can make the letters into strange shapes by distorting the grid.

Make the squares taller than they are wide...

...or wider than they are tall.

You could draw a wavy grid...

...or a curved one.

Poster tips

★ Use strong shapes and colours.
★ Don't use too many lettering styles and sizes on a poster or it will look confusing. Two or three different sorts is probably enough.
★ Attract people with a strong image and one main bit of writing. They will come closer to read the rest.

You can use this technique the other way round, to make letters smaller.

Practising big letters

Practise big letters on old newspaper or large sheets of scrap paper. Do bold, wide sweeps of your hand.

Giant-sized posters

Billboard posters are made up of several sections. You could make a huge poster yourself, out of several sheets joined together.

"Graffiti" Styles

Graffiti styles look colourful and bold. The style developed when people began spraying their names on subway trains and walls in New York in the 1960s.

It is illegal to write graffiti on walls but you can use the style on paper. It makes a vivid splash.

Inventing a tag

A tag is a graffiti writer's signature. It is usually a nickname. You could invent a tag and use it instead of signing your name. It should be striking and easy to recognize.

NiGE

A tag needs to be quick to write. The quickest sort is one colour only.

BOD-2

You could include your house number in your tag.

FLUR

This sort of tag is called a throw-up. It has an outline round a single colour.

Materials

Spray paints cover large areas quickly with flat colour. One way to copy this effect is to use marker pens. You can buy these from art shops. They are quite expensive, though, so you could try ordinary felt tips instead. The wider the tip, the better.

Marker pens

Graffiti masterpieces

Elaborate, highly-coloured, decorated bits of graffiti are known as "pieces", short for masterpieces. Here are some examples to inspire you.

This traditional style has overlapping bubble letters.

Graffiti is often painted on a cloud background.

80

Political graffiti

Sometimes people use graffiti for political or protest messages. It gets the message seen by lots of people but no one knows exactly who put it up.

This is Polish and means "solidarity".

Here are the logos of two political parties. It used to be illegal to belong to them. Graffiti styles suit the logos because members had to be secretive.

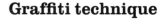

This stands for the Czechoslovakian party *Občanské Fórum* (Civic Forum).

Graffiti technique

Good graffiti needs careful planning so sketch your idea in rough before doing the real thing on paper.

1. Roughly block out the letters.

2. Add a cloud background, scenery and decoration.

3. Work out the colour scheme and fill in the colours. Use bold colours to make it look like spray paint.

4. Add a firm outline both round the letters and round the whole piece.

This complex style has a pattern of interlocking letters which can be quite difficult to read. It is called wildstyle.

3-D graffiti letters stand out well from the background.

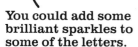

You could add some brilliant sparkles to some of the letters.

Some graffiti contains a cartoon character instead of a letter.

Magazines and newspapers

You could make your own magazine or newspaper and photocopy it for your friends and family. It looks more convincing if the articles are typewritten or word processed.

You can make headlines and titles by cutting words out of real newspapers and magazines. The words in a headline need to be the same size and style. If you can't find all the words you can make them up out of separate letters.

AUTUMN SALE

RED SOX NEWS

VIDEO VIEW

Pets Corner

Writing a news story

Newspaper stories grab your interest by telling a short version of the story in the first paragraph.

Then they go into more detail in the rest of the column.

> Club member Di Hardy had a shock last week when she was fired from her Saturday job at Spotty's pet shop.
>
> Proprietor Sam Spotworth caught Di setting mice free and smuggling a garter snake home in her pocket. Di told our reporter that the mice were overcrowded and that the snake looked ill. Red Sox have paid for the snake out of club funds. Most of the mice were caught and returned to Mr Spotworth.

Pictures

Photos and pictures help to break up the text so that it is not too dense or boring.

A colour picture will photocopy in black, white and shades of grey.

Typing columns

Justified columns in a newspaper.

Unjustified columns in this book.

Compare a newspaper with this book. The columns may look different. Columns with two straight sides are described as justified. You can justify columns on a typewriter as follows.*

Two extra spaces (one extra letter and one space between words).

> Poppy Spike's film, B
> BANANA SKIN BLUES, is
> out on video. If you
> miss it, you are a ho
> hopeless head case.

One extra space.

Three extra spaces.

Set the typewriter to a width of, for example, 21 characters. Fill each line even if you do not have room to finish a word. This will show how much extra letter space each line has.

An extra space added between each of these words.

> Poppy Spike's film,
> BANANA SKIN BLUES, is
> out on video. If you
> miss it, you are a
> hopeless head case.

One extra space added.

Three extra spaces.

Then type each line out again, adding the correct number of spaces between words to fill the whole line. Look at your first example to find out how many spaces to add to each line.

Word processors can justify text automatically.

Laying out the pages

Newspapers and magazines are laid out on a plan, or grid. This has faint lines marking the columns. It keeps the pages neat.

1. Draw a grid, such as the one on the right, on a large sheet in pale blue or yellow. (This won't show up on a photocopier.)

2. Type your columns 2mm (1/10 in) narrower than the columns on the grid.

3. Plan where each article and picture will go. Cut the columns up and stick them down on the grid.*

The first paragraph of a story can spread over two columns. Then the story divides into two columns.

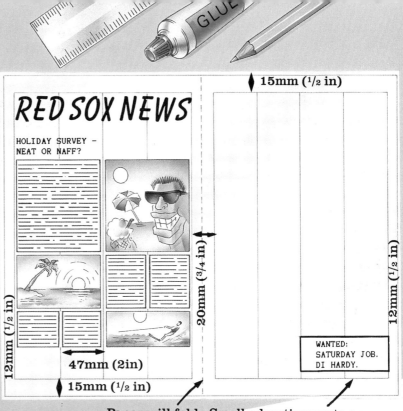

RED SOX NEWS

HOLIDAY SURVEY – NEAT OR NAFF?

WANTED:
SATURDAY JOB.
DI HARDY.

15mm (1/2 in)

20mm (3/4 in)

12mm (1/2 in)

12mm (1/2 in)

47mm (2in)

15mm (1/2 in)

Paper will fold in half here.

Small advertisements or cartoons fill odd corners.

The Geography field trip was an extravaganza of missed coaches and stolen lunches.

Spaces too big between words.

The Geograpny field trip was an extra-vaganza of missed coaches and stolen lunches.

Breaking a long word evens the lines up.

If you end up with huge gaps between words, you can use a hyphen at the end of the line. Break the word where it is easy to read it. Don't do this more than once every few lines.

Copying the paper

Most photocopiers let you copy on to both sides of the paper. If you print on both sides of a large sheet and fold it in half, you end up with a four-page magazine or newspaper.

1. Paste up two sheets like this:

Back page 4	Front page 1

Page 2	Page 3

2. Photocopy pages 4 and 1.

Follow these stages so that the pages end up in the right order. Not all photocopiers behave the same so read the instructions and expect a few trial runs.

3. Put pages 2-3 in the copier ready for copying.

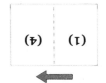

4. Feed the copy of pages 4 and 1 in upside down and blank side up.

*The process of sticking the text and pictures on the grid is called paste-up.

Illuminating letters

In the Middle Ages, monks copying out books often decorated the first letter of a page or paragraph. This is called illumination.

Books were very rare and precious in those days. Monks used beautiful colours and even gold leaf to make the letters shine. You could do an illuminated letter at the beginning of a story or important message.

Boxed letters

Draw a faint box outline in hard pencil. Then sketch the letter outline inside.

You could colour the letter like this...

...or use details from a story.

Free letters

An illuminated letter can fill a whole page. You could make a card for someone by illuminating their initial. You could shape a message around it.

Modern styles

It is quite fun to mix this ancient technique with a modern lettering style. You could begin a letter to a friend with a big greeting.

Magazine style

Magazines often use a large initial letter to make a page look more interesting.

There is a gothic alphabet to copy or trace on page 94.

Tips

★ Try to make the letter as easy to read as possible.
★ The style of the rest of the writing should match the illuminated letter. Try gothic style if you want an ancient feel.*

Materials

A hard pencil is best for sketching decoration. You could use crayons, felt-tips or watercolour paint for colouring in.

You can buy gold and silver paint and pens from art shops. Metallic paint loses its shine with age, though.

Lettering on fabric

If you buy paints for fabrics, you can write on T-shirts, banners and flags. Some fabric paints can only be used on natural materials such as cotton, so check the instructions. Check that the paint is washable, too.

T-shirt art

Bold, black letters on white T-shirts look very striking.

This style is often used for protest messages.

Work out your design on paper. Peg the T-shirt flat on a stiff board and copy the design in pale-coloured chalk. To do an exact copy, use the grid technique described on page 79. Now paint in the design. The chalk outline will soon wear off or wash out.

Practical tips

For crisp letter outlines, wear down the chalk to give it a sharp edge.

You could mix coloured pictures and letters.

Put paper between the layers of fabric to stop paint seeping through - not newspaper, though, as the print rubs off.

Printing on fabric

You can make fabric printing blocks using the techniques shown on pages 88–89. Use fabric paint or fabric printing ink, available from art shops.

You can repeat letter designs to create larger printed patterns.

Stretch the fabric out flat, as you did with the T-shirt.

Flags and banners

It is hard to read letters on flags so use short words. You could fly a flag outside on your birthday with your age on it. For longer messages, you could do lots of single letters across a stretch of bunting.

Try drawing a banner in miniature first. This makes it easier to work out the design. For example, if your banner is to be 3m (10ft) long, scale it down to 30cm (1ft). Use the grid technique (see page 79) to copy the design in chalk before painting it in.

Handwriting styles

Everyone's handwriting is different. It is as individual as your voice. Whatever its shape, though, it is important that it is easy to read. Some people practise handwriting as an art. This is called calligraphy.

The art of calligraphy

Calligraphy is based on traditional handwriting styles. Two calligraphy styles, roman and italic, are shown below.

> Roman calligraphy has developed over 2000 years. It is upright, with rounded letters.

> *Italic writing was devised about 500 years ago. It slopes gracefully to the right.*

Making large letters

You can draw large, italic style letter outlines using a twin-pointed pencil. To make one, tape two pencils tightly together.

The pencil points act like the edges of a nib.

Fill in the letters using a paintbrush.

Forming italic letters

Most italic letters are made up of several separate strokes. Take your pen off the paper between each stroke. Below are some letters to try. You can find out about italic pens on page 69 and there is an italic alphabet to copy on page 95.

You will need to use a flat-tipped italic nib.* Hold it at the correct angle (see page 69).

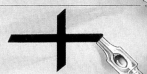

Diagonal lines are thick or thin depending on which way your pen is moving.

Form rounded shapes in two separate strokes.

Arched strokes branch from about half way up the stem.

You need to do the pen strokes in the order and direction shown by the arrows.

Small finishing strokes are called serifs. To make these, push the pen up slightly before and after downward strokes.

For coloured calligraphy, try using either diluted poster paint or coloured inks.

*There are specially designed calligraphy nibs for left-handers.

Another calligraphy style

Copperplate is a sort of italic style that was used for carving into glass or metal. On paper, people used quill pens which gave a thicker stroke when pressed harder.

You can try copperplate using any thin nib. Do continuous, sweeping strokes keeping the pen on the paper. You can thicken downstrokes afterwards.

Swirls and flourishes

You can decorate calligraphy with flowing

Copperplate engraving on a silver tankard.

Letters flow into each other.

swirls, called flourishes. Here are some examples.

Make strokes in steady, continuous sweeps.

Pull the pen towards you for sloping lines.

You and your signature

To develop your signature, try writing your name very fast several times. Which bits feel easiest and how can you exaggerate them? Play with your signature like a design.

Some people think that your signature gives a clue to what you are like. Here are some signatures with different characteristics.

Romantic

Aggressive

Decisive

Handwriting secrets

Some people believe that you can tell what a person is like from their handwriting. This is called graphology. Below are some of the things graphologists look for in handwriting.

Tall ascenders are supposed to show imagination. *grandly*

Someone whose writing is very large in the middle area is supposed to be big-headed. *grandly*

Big, curvy descenders may mean that a person is very athletic. *grandly*

The slant of a person's writing is supposed to reflect their confidence.

Left slant: shy and private. *funny*

Right slant: outgoing and sociable. *funny*

Upright: self-controlled. *funny*

If a person's writing slopes either up or down the page, this is supposed to indicate their mood.

Eager & enthusiastic

Tired and bored

Printing letters

These two pages show you how to make printing blocks so that you can repeat your lettering again and again.

You could use this idea to make a personalized logo or your own slogan to use on cards and letters.

Making a printing block

You can make a printing block out of anything that is easy to carve, such as a lump of polystyrene or soft cork. You could make one out of a hard vegetable like a potato – but remember that a vegetable will go bad after a few days.

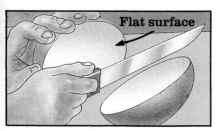
Flat surface

First, you need to cut the block so that it has a flat surface.

Draw a letter backwards on to the surface so it will print the right way round.

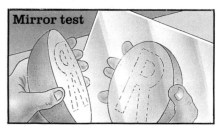
Mirror test

This is tricky so check the letter in a mirror before you cut it out.

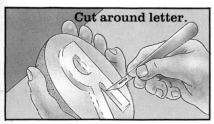
Cut around letter.

Using a pointed knife, carve around the letter so that its shape is raised up. Cut out any spaces within the letter too.

Press down firmly.
Coat with paint.

Next, brush some paint or ink on to a flat plate. Press the printing block on to the paint to cover the surface of the letter.

Finally, press the block firmly on to the paper. Make sure the block does not slip sideways as this will smudge the letter.

Texture and colour

Printing blocks made from different materials can create unusual effects. You could experiment with different textures and coloured paints. Here are some ideas.

88 *Oasis is used for flower arranging. You can buy it from flower shops.*

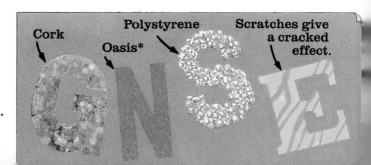
Cork
Oasis*
Polystyrene
Scratches give a cracked effect.

More printing blocks

Another way to make a printing block is to glue a letter shape on to a piece of wood. The surface has to be flat and the letter needs to be made out of something raised, such as string or corrugated cardboard.

Remember to draw letters in reverse and do the mirror test before you cut or glue.

Cut out the letter shape or form it out of string.

Glue the letter firmly on to the wood.

When the glue is dry, coat the letter with paint and print it (see opposite page).

Famous monograms

Yves
Saint Laurent

Volkswagen

Coco Chanel

Rolls Royce

Designs made out of letters are called monograms.
  Companies sometimes create monograms from their initials so that people will remember their names. Here are some famous monograms. You could try making a design out of your own initials.

Printed letter designs

By repeating letter shapes you can form intricate patterns and pictures.

Letter shapes

If you want to print a longer message, you can avoid cutting out every letter by making blocks for basic letter shapes.

Below are the four shapes you will need. You can combine them upside down and both ways round to make letters.

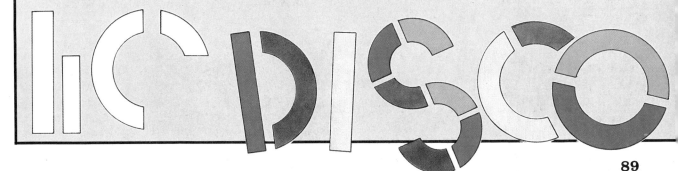

STENCILLING

Stencils are sheets of plastic or card with shapes cut out. You draw round or paint inside the shapes. You can create perfect lettering quickly and easily using a set of ready-made letter stencils. These come in various sizes.

Below are some different ways to use letter stencils.

You can buy large stencils for big lettering.

Sets of stencils usually include capitals, small letters and numbers.

Outline stencilling.

Filled-in stencilling

Stencils made of tough plastic can be cleaned and used again and again.

Stencilling with a brush

With a set of large letter stencils, you can create various textures using a stencil brush. These are sold at art shops. They are thick with stiff bristles.

Mix some fairly thick paint and dip the brush tips into it. Wipe the brush on spare paper until it is almost dry.

Hold the brush upright and stencil right to the edge.

Hold the stencil firmly and dab the brush lightly over the letter. A few dabs give a dotty texture. The more you go over the letter, the smoother the texture becomes.

You could overlap the letters.

Too much paint causes splats.

You could stencil letters on to coloured paper or fade one colour into another.

Other stencilling ideas

These stencilling methods are quite messy so you will need to cover up everything except the letter you want.

Splattering paint with a paintbrush.

Dabbing thick paint on with a sponge.

Flicking paint from an old toothbrush.

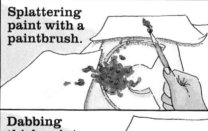
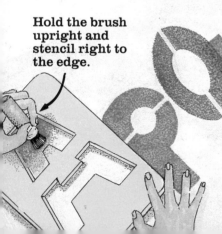

Creative photocopying

Photocopiers are being used more and more by artists and designers. They can help you to create dramatic effects, correct mistakes and produce lots of copies of your finished lettering. Some can copy in colour.

Enlarging and reducing

Many photocopiers can make things larger or smaller. If you reduce lettering (make it smaller), smudges and wobbles become smaller too, so the letters look neater. By enlarging lettering you can make it look worn (see page 70).

Photocopiers enlarge or reduce by percentages. Many machines copy down to half-size (50%) and up to double size (200%). To make letters very big or small, you need to enlarge or reduce them many times.

Fancy lettering looks very precise if you reduce it.

You could do the last copy on to coloured paper.

3-D lettering

Modelling clay letters on the copier.

Using a photocopier, you can create flat lettering out of all kinds of solid objects. The copier copies shadows too, so the effect is 3-D. Because you see the back of the letters when you put them face-down on the copier, remember to form words back to front.

Multiple copies

If you are making cards or invitations, here is a quick way to make lots of copies.

Fold a piece of copier paper in four sections and do your lettering in one section.

Take a copy, cut it out and stick it next to the original.

Make a second copy and stick this underneath the first two.

You can use this master copy to print your hand-lettered invitations four at a time.

Correcting mistakes

To correct black and white lettering, stick a small piece of white paper over the error. Now take a copy and try again. If the patch shows, adjust the tone control for a lighter copy.

1. Error

2. Small patch.

3. Try again on a copy.

Layout and presentation

When information is well laid out and attractively presented, it is more enjoyable to read and easier to understand. These two pages give some advice on how you could present a school project. Many of the same tips are useful, though, whatever you are presenting.

Textured paper can clog up ink pens.

Patterned paper can make writing hard to read.

Some typewriters won't take thick paper.

Make sure your writing will show up if you use dark coloured paper.

Mistakes can be hard to correct on coloured paper.

Choosing your paper

Before you start writing up your project, you need to decide what paper to use. Bear in mind whether the project will be hand-written or typed: it needs to look clear and neat on the paper you use.

Introducing your project

The first pages of a document are called the "preliminaries". They should introduce the subject and make people interested in what they are about to read.

The cover should be eye-catching. It should display the title of the project and your name. You could add pictures which say something about the subject.

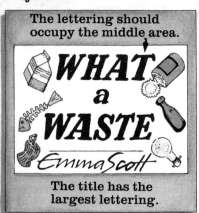

The lettering should occupy the middle area.

The title has the largest lettering.

Lettering should be smaller than on the cover.

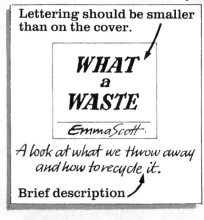

WHAT a WASTE — Emma Scott

A look at what we throw away and how to recycle it.

Brief description

The next page is the first page of your project. It is called the title page. Repeat the project's name and your own. You could also add a brief description of the project.

Next, there should be a list of contents. This should include all the sections in the project and give their page numbers. The title and contents list can go on the same page if you like.

You could position the contents off-centre.

Contents

Make sure page numbers are not too far from their sections.

— 2
— 4
— 6
— 8
— 10
— 12
— 14
— 16

Laying out the pages

The layout of a page makes a lot of difference to how easy it is to read. An untidy or cramped page can be confusing.

Spaces make people pause and help them to absorb a piece of information before moving on to the next.

Headings have the largest lettering on the page. They introduce major new sections.

Sub-headings should stand out. They break the section into smaller topics and make it easier to absorb.

Leave plenty of space between lines and paragraphs.

Leave wide margins and generous spaces top and bottom of a page.

Borders and motifs can add colour. Make sure they do not dominate the page though.

Illustrations should have lots of room. A large picture could have a whole page to itself.

Captions go underneath pictures or to one side.

Page numbers should be clear. The odd numbers go on the right hand page.

SPACE FLIGHT
Orbiting Satellites

6 — 7

Ways to bind your project

You will need a binding to hold the pages of your project together. Take into account the number of pages and thickness of the paper when you choose a binding.

Ribbon can look elegant. Tie it quite loosely, though, or it will be hard to open the pages.

Around Our Town

You can have a project spiral-bound at a quick-print shop.

Cardboard at the back stops pages from getting crumpled.

A sheet of clear plastic protects the cover.

My Life So Far

You can buy slide binders from stationery shops.

You could hold a small project together with staples.

You can protect punched holes with reinforcers from a stationery shop.

BATS

Alphabets to copy

Here are four alphabets for you to trace or copy. You can enlarge the letters using the grid technique explained on page 79.

Roman

ABCDEFGHIJKLM
NOPQRSTUVWXYZ
abcdefghijklmnopqrst
uvwxyz 1234567890

Gothic

ABCDEFGHIJKLM
NOPQRSTUVWXYZ
abcdefghijklmnopqrstuvwxyz
1234567890

Serif and non-serif alphabets

These four alphabets are serif alphabets, that is, the letters have finishing strokes. Letters without serifs, like those over the page, are called sans-serif, or non-serif, letters.

Italic

ABCDEFGHIJKLM
NOPQRSTUVWXYZ
abcdefghijklmnopqrstuv
wxyz 1234567890

Art Nouveau

ABCDEFGHIJKLM
NOPQRSTUVWXYZ
abcdefghijklmnopqrstuv
wxyz 1234567890

These two alphabets are sans-serif. The
first looks plain. The alphabet at the
bottom looks more unusual.

ABCDEFGHIJKLM
NOPQRSTUVWXYZ
abcdefghijklmnopqrst
uvwxyz 1234567890

ABCDEFGHIJKLM
NOPQRSTUVWXYZ
abcdefghijklmnopqrs
tuvwxyz 1234567890

Part Four
HOW TO DRAW
SPACECRAFT

Emma Fischel and Anita Ganeri

Designed by Mike Pringle, Steve Page,
Brian Robertson, Richard Maddox,
Kim Blundell and Chris Gillingwater

Illustrated by Mike Pringle, Gary Mayes,
Guy Smith, Martin Newton, Kim Blundell
and Kuo Kang Chen

Contents

About part four

Part four shows you how to draw things associated with space. As well as spacecraft and other space machines, you can see how to draw planet landscapes, aliens, astronauts and future worlds.

Space machines

In this part there are many ideas for drawing real space machines, from rockets and space telescopes to satellites and space stations. You can see how to use similar ideas to draw imaginary spacecraft. There are also suggestions for drawing robots and Unidentified Flying Objects (UFOs).

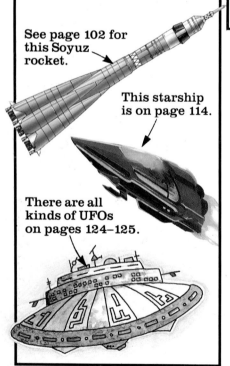

See page 102 for this Soyuz rocket.

This starship is on page 114.

There are all kinds of UFOs on pages 124–125.

Drawing backgrounds

A dramatic background can really help make your picture stand out on the page. There are many suggestions for ways of creating atmospheric backgrounds, such as using the comets and meteors on pages 104–105 or planets from page 106.

Fantasy drawing

As space is still largely unexplored, there is plenty of scope for using your imagination to create pictures of life in the future. Pages 114–117 show what life might be like on a planet in the 21st century. On pages 120–123 you can see examples of fantasy and comic strip art done by science fiction artists, with tips on drawing your own fantasy pictures.

Drawing tips

Drawing in stages

Many of the pictures have step-by-step outlines to help you draw them. Sketch all the outlines in pencil first.

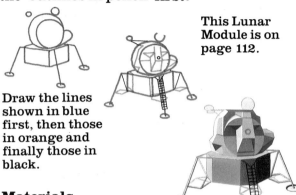

This Lunar Module is on page 112.

Draw the lines shown in blue first, then those in orange and finally those in black.

Materials

Airbrushing is explained on pages 102 and 106.

There are many suggestions for colouring materials to use. Some pictures are done with an airbrush. Airbrushes used by professionals can be expensive but you can buy cheaper models from art shops.

Professional techniques

This book gives many examples of techniques used by designers to show how parts of a space machine work or fit together. By following the simple explanations you can see how to give your drawings a really professional look.

There are cutaways on pages 108 and 110–111.

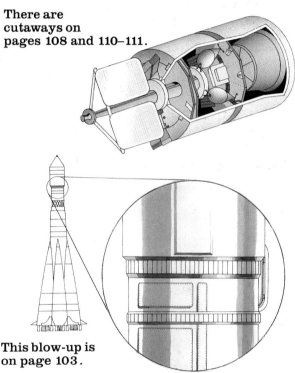

This blow-up is on page 103.

Mixing pictures

You could combine realistic and fantasy pictures from this book to create original space scenes. In this picture, for example, realistic astronauts come face to face with an alien on an imaginary planet.

Rockets

On the following four pages there are many different kinds of rockets to draw, from the first rocket to take men to the Moon, to the Space Shuttle. You can also find out about colouring and design techniques used by professional artists.

Drawing a rocket

The rocket on the right can be broken down into fairly simple shapes. Use the steps below to help you draw it. Sketch the outlines in pencil first so you get the shapes right. Make the rocket any size you like.

1 Draw the lines shown in pencil first. These are called construction lines. They will help you position the shapes correctly and make them the right size in relation to each other. Next, draw the lines shown in blue.

Construction lines are just a guide, not part of the finished picture.

2 Draw in the lines shown in orange. Then add the details shown in black. Go over the finished outline in fine black felt tip, then rub out the construction lines.

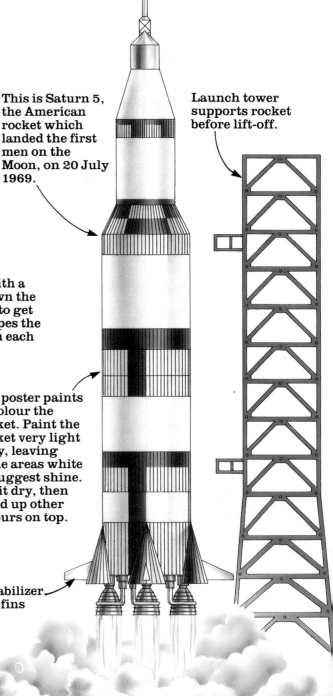

This is Saturn 5, the American rocket which landed the first men on the Moon, on 20 July 1969.

Launch tower supports rocket before lift-off.

Start with a line down the middle to get the shapes the same on each side.

Use poster paints to colour the rocket. Paint the rocket very light grey, leaving some areas white to suggest shine. Let it dry, then build up other colours on top.

Stabilizer fins

100

Using a grid

If you want to copy a spacecraft picture from a magazine, book or photograph but would like to make it a different size from the original, try this grid method.

1 Draw a grid of equal-sized squares on tracing paper. Make the grid big enough to cover the picture you want to copy.

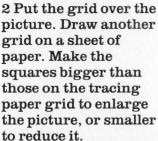

2 Put the grid over the picture. Draw another grid on a sheet of paper. Make the squares bigger than those on the tracing paper grid to enlarge the picture, or smaller to reduce it.

3 Look at each square on the tracing paper grid and copy the shape in it on to the same square on your second grid. Lastly, rub out the grid lines.

The Space Shuttle

The first Space Shuttle was launched by the USA in 1981. A Shuttle takes off like a rocket but lands horizontally, like a plane. Its fuel tanks are jettisoned (released) once the fuel is used up. To draw the picture below, first copy the shape in the box.

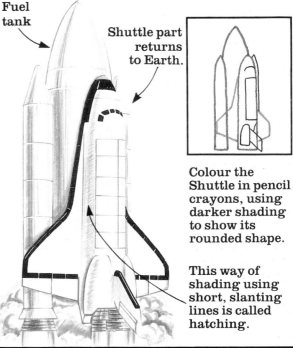

Fuel tank

Shuttle part returns to Earth.

Colour the Shuttle in pencil crayons, using darker shading to show its rounded shape.

This way of shading using short, slanting lines is called hatching.

Cartoon rockets

To draw these cartoon rockets, copy the shapes in pencil then go over the outlines in black felt tip. Use bright colours to fill in the shapes.

   Rockets need to travel very fast to go into space. They reach speeds of at least 40,000km/h (25,000mph).

If a rocket does not go fast enough, it falls back to Earth.

101

Drawing a Soyuz rocket

This picture is of a Russian Soyuz rocket. Soyuz has been used to launch manned space capsules into orbit. Use the steps below to help you draw the rocket.

The picture has been airbrushed. Airbrushing is a technique often used by professional artists. You can see how it is done in the box below.

Space capsule

1 Pencil in construction lines to help position the parts of the rocket. * Draw the shapes shown in blue. 2 Next, draw the shapes shown in orange, then those shown in black.

A combination of pale and darker streaks shows the shine on the body and makes the rocket look 3-dimensional.

Launch section

Fine black lines make details stand out clearly.

The first Soyuz rocket was launched on 23 April 1967. The latest Soyuz was launched on 7 June 1988.

Using an airbrush

Artists use airbrushing to produce pictures that look almost like photographs.

An airbrush looks like a fat fountain pen with a tube attached to it. Air is pushed through the tube and forces paint out of a nozzle at the end of the airbrush. The air flow must be regular so the paint flows smoothly.

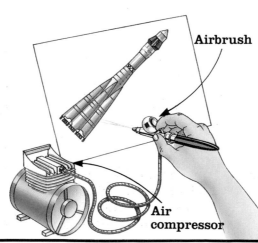

Airbrush

Air compressor

Airbrushing is popular with artists who draw machines. It is good for showing a smooth metallic finish on a machine with different tones of the same colour. An airbrush can also produce fine lines and solid blocks of even colour.

Blow-ups

The picture below shows a blow-up. Professional designers use this technique to pull out one part of a machine and show it in a lot of detail. To draw this blow-up, follow the steps below.

1 First draw the outline of the whole rocket in pencil. Draw a small circle round the part to be blown up.

2 Draw two straight lines extending from the circle, then draw a larger circle between them.

This blow-up shows details of the Russian Vostok spacecraft.

You could use a different shape to frame the blow-up, such as a square or rectangle.

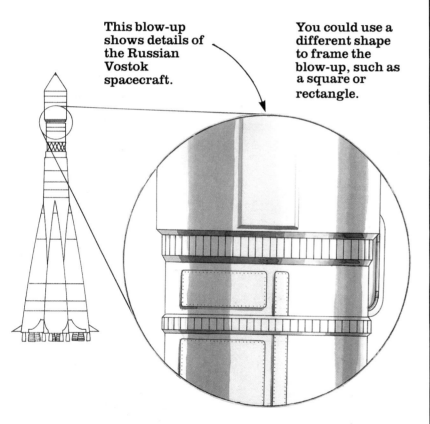

3 Next, fill in the details of the part that is blown up inside the circle frame.

4 Go over the pencil lines in black felt tip. Then use blue and grey watercolour to paint the blow-up.

Exploded drawings

Exploded drawings are used to show how parts of a machine fit together. Parts are drawn slightly away from their true position to show how they are joined to each other.

This picture is of Apollo 11.

Arrows show exactly where the parts fit together.

Use long strokes of pencil crayon for the outer shell.

Try working out your own exploded drawings using the ideas above. You could use some of the machines shown later in this book, such as the space telescope on page 109 or the lunar module on page 112.

Space journey

Here you can see how to draw the various stages of a rocket's journey through space.* There are also tips on creating the dramatic background.

Perspective

Rocket zooming into space.

Objects look smaller the further away they are. This is called perspective.

Escape tower

Stars are grouped in giant clusters called galaxies.

Third stage

A rocket built in one piece would be too heavy to gain enough speed to enter space.

Second stage

First stage jettisoned.

Meteors are small pieces of rock. At about 80km (50 miles) from Earth they burn up, making streaks of light called shooting stars.

First stage

A multi-stage rocket

Rockets are used to launch satellites and manned spacecraft into space. As rockets need to reach huge speeds in order to enter space (see page 101), they are built in sections, called stages. Each stage is jettisoned when its fuel is used up, making the rest of the rocket lighter and faster. The next stage's engines fire, giving the rocket more power and speed.

*See page 100 for a rocket's basic shape.

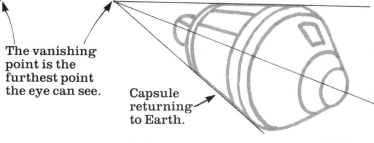

The vanishing point is the furthest point the eye can see.

Capsule returning to Earth.

To draw these spacecraft in perspective, first draw three lines meeting at a point.

This is called the vanishing point. Draw in the shapes between the lines.

Distances in space are so huge that they are measured in light years. A light year is the distance light travels in a year, about 9.5 million million km (6 million million miles).

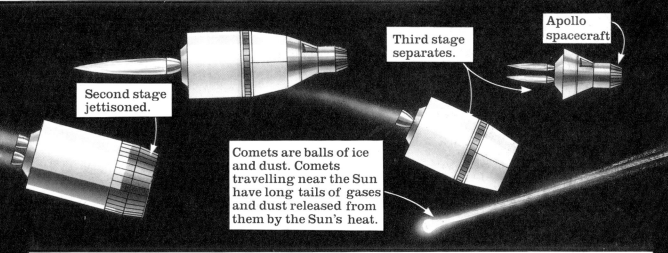

Second stage jettisoned.

Third stage separates.

Apollo spacecraft

Comets are balls of ice and dust. Comets travelling near the Sun have long tails of gases and dust released from them by the Sun's heat.

Drawing the background

Here are some suggestions for ways to colour in a space background, using a mixture of watercolours and chalks on a sheet of dark blue or black paper.

To draw star clusters, dip a brush into white paint. Flick the paint on to the paper with your finger.* Add crosses and smudges of chalk.

Draw the comets in white paint. Use a thick splodge of paint for the body. Then add quite thick, dry streaks for the tail.

To draw meteors, start by painting the shapes white. Let this dry, then add layers of light and dark brown paint on top.

*Cover up the rest of the picture to protect it from splashes.

The planets

Earth is in a part of space called the Solar System. This is made up of the Sun, nine planets which orbit it, their moons and a band of rocks called asteroids. Below you can find out more about planets and ways of drawing them.

Venus

The Sun

Asteroid belt

Earth

Mercury

Saturn

The daytime temperature on Mercury can reach 350°C.

Mars

The time a planet takes to orbit the Sun once is called its "year".

Uranus

Neptune

Jupiter

Pluto

Lines show path of planet's orbit.

Professional tip

The picture above was drawn with an airbrush.* Only one colour can be put on at a time so an artist uses "masks" to protect the rest of the painting that is not being sprayed.

Masks can be made of card or film, or masking fluid may be used. This is painted on and can be peeled off later. To get sharp, clear edges an artist uses a card stencil and sprays the area inside it.

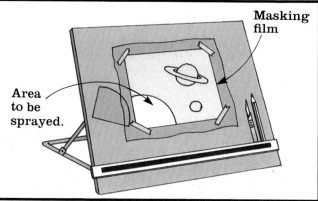

Masking film

Area to be sprayed.

Drawing the planets

If you don't have an airbrush you can achieve dramatic effects using shades of pencil crayons.

Jupiter

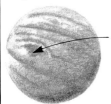

The red patch is a huge hurricane, about three times as big as Earth.

Use pale red and orange with darker bands on top. Add shadows round the bottom half of the planet.

Saturn

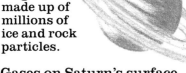

Saturn's rings are made up of millions of ice and rock particles.

Gases on Saturn's surface make bands of different colours. Show this with contrasting shades.

Uranus

Uranus takes 84 Earth years to orbit the Sun.

Uranus looks green because of clouds of methane gas swirling around it. Shade this with green and yellow.

Planetary probes

Planetary probes are unmanned spacecraft, launched into space by rockets. Cameras on board send back pictures of planets' surfaces.

Mariner

Here you can see how to draw the probe Mariner 4, which took photographs of the surface of Mars.

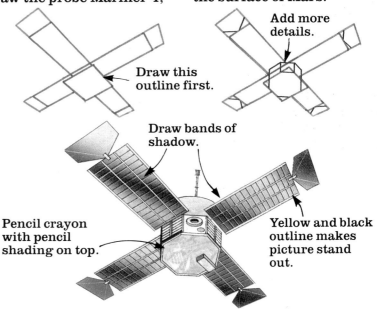

Draw this outline first.

Add more details.

Draw bands of shadow.

Pencil crayon with pencil shading on top.

Yellow and black outline makes picture stand out.

Surface of Mars

Use yellow to show clouds.

Mars is called the Red Planet because its surface is made up of rusty-red rocks. Dust from them also makes the sky look pink.

Use pencil crayons for Mars' surface and watercolours for the sky.

Looking at space

A satellite is any object in space which orbits a larger object. It can be natural, like Earth which orbits the Sun, or artificial, like the ones on these pages.

Comstar 1

To draw this picture of Comstar 1, first copy the outline shapes below in pencil. Colour the body with felt tips and add the final details with fine black lines.

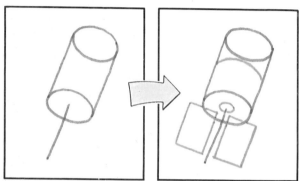

Use quite thick felt tips for the planet.

A white area suggests a metal shine on the satellite.

Drawing a cutaway

This picture is called a cutaway. Cutaways leave out part of a machine's outer shell to show what is inside it.* They are often used by spacecraft designers to show how the equipment on board is to be carried.

To draw this cutaway, pencil in the outline of the satellite's shell and draw a line round the area which will form the cutaway section. Add more details to both sections, then go over the pencil lines in black. Colour the satellite with felt tips.

Comstar 1 is a communications satellite.

Radio equipment beams signals from one place to another.

To show the contrast between the two parts, you could colour in one section only and just outline the other.

The white line shows the cutaway section.

*See how to draw a cutaway space station on page 110.

Satellites at work

Satellites are used mainly for weather forecasting and communications. They can take pictures of cloud patterns, for example, or beam television signals from one place to another.

This cartoon shows satellites which are geo-stationary (staying in a fixed place high above the Equator) and polar orbiting (circling Earth between the poles).

Draw the cartoon in pencil first, then colour the satellites with bright felt tips and go over the outlines in black. Colour Earth in green and blue felt tips. Add quite dry, thick white paint on top for clouds.

Polar orbiting satellite.

Geo-stationary satellite.

Arrows show position of satellites in relation to Earth.

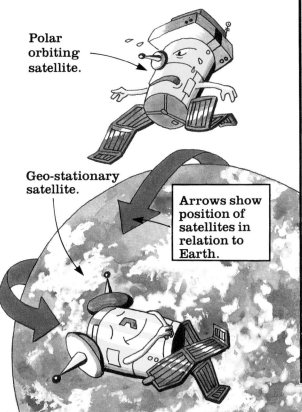

Space telescope

This is a telescope the USA plans to launch into space. It can see seven times further than any other telescope ever built.

A telescope like this in London, England could see a coin in Frankfurt, Germany, about 700km (440 miles) away.

Make areas darker by drawing the dots closer together.

To draw the telescope, start by copying the outline shape shown on the right. Shade the body in pencil, using small dots. This technique is called stippling and is a good way of suggesting the curved surfaces of a machine.

Draw the lines shown in blue, then orange, then black.

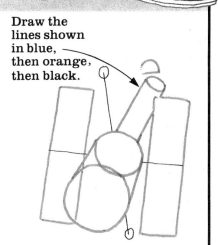

Inside a space station

A space station is a type of satellite launched by a rocket. It carries a crew and equipment for doing scientific research impossible to do on Earth. It also studies how people are affected by spending a long time in space.

Skylab

Skylab was launched in 1973. Amongst other equipment, it carried a telescope to study the Sun.

Here you can see how to draw this cutaway of Skylab by breaking it down into simple shapes. Start by copying the blue outline.

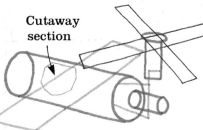

The basic body shapes are cylinders.

Next, add the lines shown in orange and black. Pencil in the outline of the part of Skylab to be cut away.

Cutaway section

Add further details from the main picture on the right. Draw over the pencil lines in black, then use poster paints or pencil crayons to colour it in.

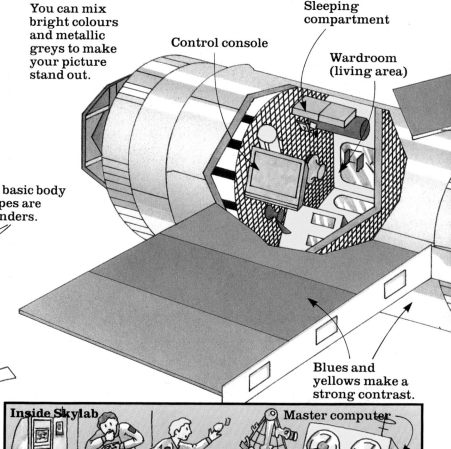

You can mix bright colours and metallic greys to make your picture stand out.

Sleeping compartment

Control console

Wardroom (living area)

Blues and yellows make a strong contrast.

Inside Skylab

Master computer

Astronauts eating

You could use a cartoon style to draw some aspects of life on board Skylab. Use bright colours and black outlines to make the cartoons stand out.

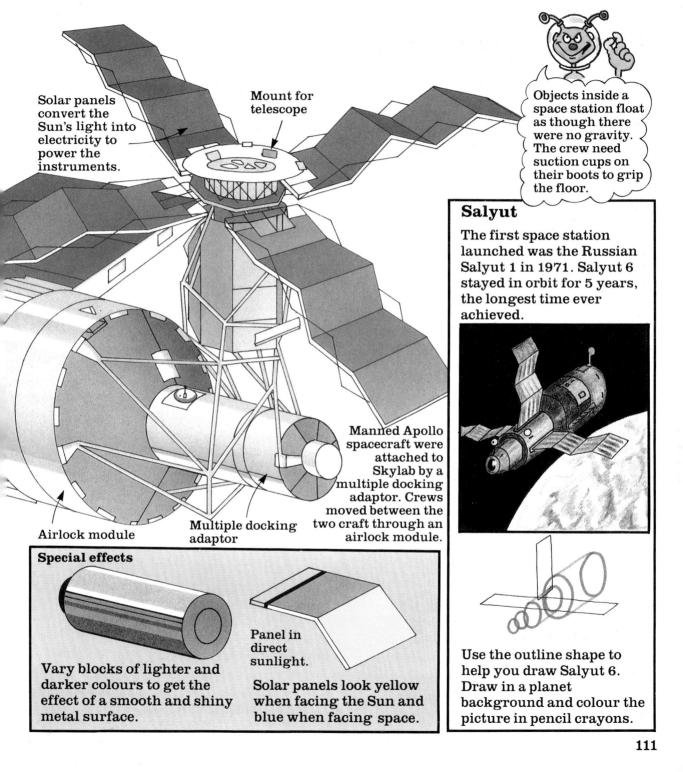

Solar panels convert the Sun's light into electricity to power the instruments.

Mount for telescope

Objects inside a space station float as though there were no gravity. The crew need suction cups on their boots to grip the floor.

Salyut

The first space station launched was the Russian Salyut 1 in 1971. Salyut 6 stayed in orbit for 5 years, the longest time ever achieved.

Airlock module

Multiple docking adaptor

Manned Apollo spacecraft were attached to Skylab by a multiple docking adaptor. Crews moved between the two craft through an airlock module.

Special effects

Vary blocks of lighter and darker colours to get the effect of a smooth and shiny metal surface.

Panel in direct sunlight.

Solar panels look yellow when facing the Sun and blue when facing space.

Use the outline shape to help you draw Salyut 6. Draw in a planet background and colour the picture in pencil crayons.

On the Moon

The Moon is over 380,000km away, but it is Earth's closest neighbour in space. Since unmanned lunar probes were launched in the 1950s, man has landed on the Moon and we now know more about what it looks like. Here you can see how to draw the Moon's surface and machines which have landed on it.

Lunar Module

To enlarge this shape you could use a grid (see page 101).

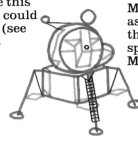

The Lunar Module took astronauts from the USA Apollo spacecraft to the Moon's surface.

To draw the Lunar Module, follow the outlines above. Draw the lines shown in blue first.

Next, draw the lines shown in orange, then add the further details shown in black to your picture.

Fill in the shapes with bright blocks of colour. To make the picture stand out further, you could outline it in black.

The Lunar Rover was transported to the Moon by Apollo 15 in 1971.

The first man on the Moon was Neil Armstrong. He landed on 20 July 1969.

The surface of the Moon is very dry and dusty. To get the grainy look, put a sheet of sandpaper under your picture when you colour it.

Moon craters

The surface of the Moon is pitted with millions of craters. These were probably caused by meteorites crashing on to its surface.

From the Moon, Earth seems to change shape. This is because often only part of it can be seen.

The Module was covered in a substance like foil to protect it from the Sun's intense heat, so colour it silver.

Astronauts bounce along the ground because gravity on the Moon is six times less than on Earth, so they are six times lighter.

There is no wind or rain on the Moon, so astronauts' footprints will never be worn away.

Use pencil crayons to draw the craters. To show the insides, use dark pencil shading and white highlights.

Spacesuits

As the Moon has no air, astronauts have to wear special suits with tanks providing them with oxygen to breathe. The suits also protect them from the cold on the Moon.

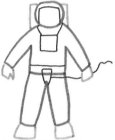

Use the outline above to help you draw this astronaut.

Colour the spacesuit in watercolour paint. Use highlights to show the shine on the material.

113

The future in space

This picture shows what life might be like on an imaginary planet in the year 2090 AD. Although this is a fantasy picture, many of the things in it are based on scientific theory about advances that may be possible by then.

The picture is done in airbrush and gouache (a type of poster paint used by professional artists). Over the page there are suggestions for drawing some of the objects shown here and tips on creating some of the special effects.

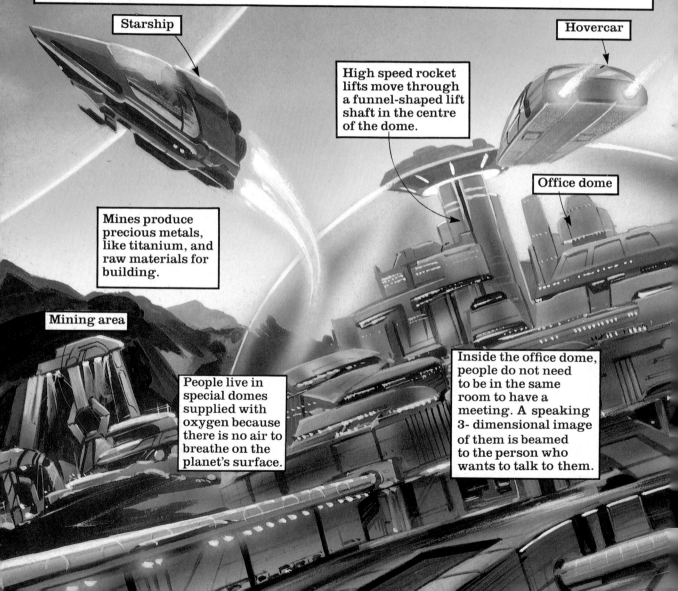

Starship

Hovercar

High speed rocket lifts move through a funnel-shaped lift shaft in the centre of the dome.

Office dome

Mines produce precious metals, like titanium, and raw materials for building.

Mining area

People live in special domes supplied with oxygen because there is no air to breathe on the planet's surface.

Inside the office dome, people do not need to be in the same room to have a meeting. A speaking 3-dimensional image of them is beamed to the person who wants to talk to them.

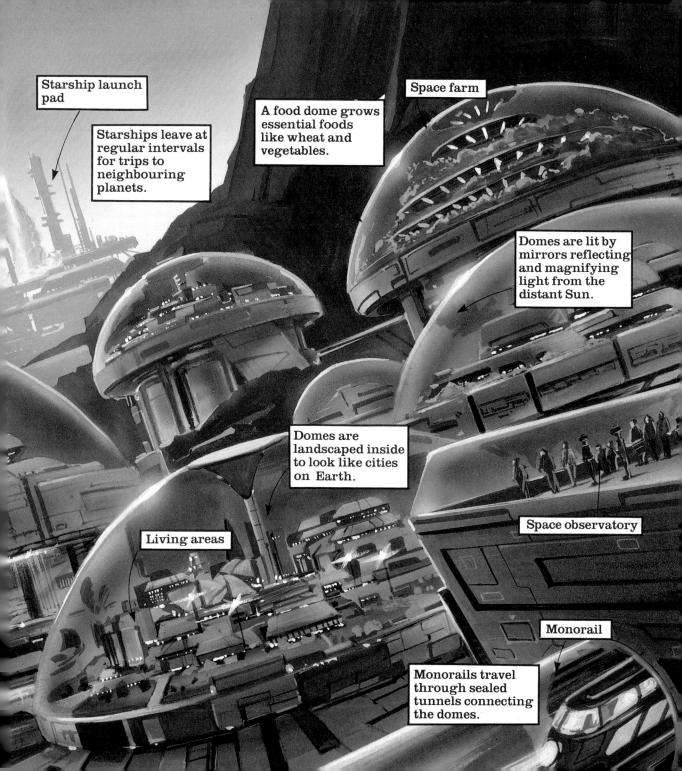

Starship launch pad

Starships leave at regular intervals for trips to neighbouring planets.

A food dome grows essential foods like wheat and vegetables.

Space farm

Domes are lit by mirrors reflecting and magnifying light from the distant Sun.

Domes are landscaped inside to look like cities on Earth.

Living areas

Space observatory

Monorail

Monorails travel through sealed tunnels connecting the domes.

Transport in the future

Here are three forms of transport that might be used on a planet in the 21st century. Follow the outlines and the tips below to help you draw these vehicles.

Hovercar

Colour the hovercar in soft pencil crayons, adding a logo to its roof.*

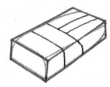

Logo

An automatic navigator on board works out the best route.

Starship

Leaving white gaps along the body helps give an impression of great speed.

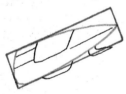

Streamlined shape designed to produce maximum speed.

Monorail

Suggest the shiny glass of the windows by using blue and white crayons.

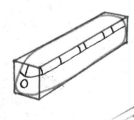

Uses a single runner instead of wheels.

For the background use long crayon strokes. Smudge the colours with your finger to blend them together.

*There are more logo ideas on page 126.

Painting tips

Below are some tips on how to draw the space scene on the previous page.

Paint nearer objects darker and use paler colours for things in the distance.

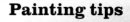

Use white for the dome

A thick blob suggests the reflecting mirror which lights the dome.

Dabs of yellow paint look like tiny windows

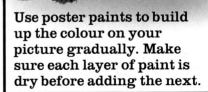

Use poster paints to build up the colour on your picture gradually. Make sure each layer of paint is dry before adding the next.

Drawing a robot

By the year 2090 AD robots could be a common feature in the home. To draw this robot, start by copying the shapes below.

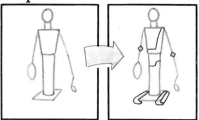

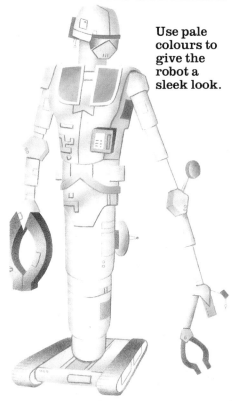

Use pale colours to give the robot a sleek look.

Go over the details in black to show all the parts of the robot clearly.

Inside a 21st century house

This picture shows what a typical room might look like in 2090. Draw the basic shapes in the room before adding further details. Use poster paints to colour it, with pencil crayon lines on top for extra shading.

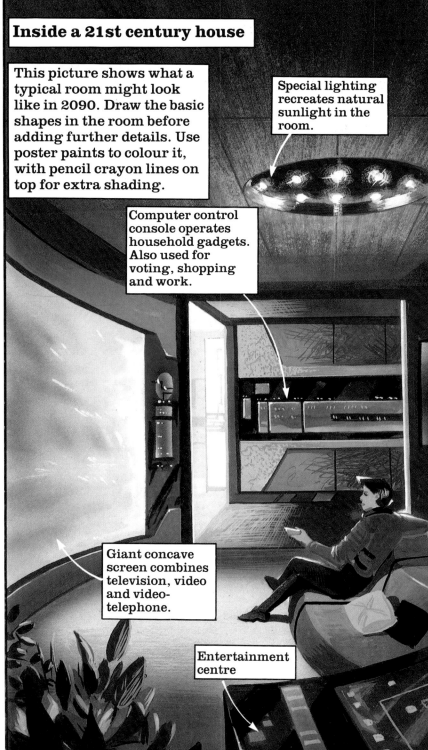

Special lighting recreates natural sunlight in the room.

Computer control console operates household gadgets. Also used for voting, shopping and work.

Giant concave screen combines television, video and video-telephone.

Entertainment centre

Space aliens

Space travel has not been able to prove that life exists on other planets – yet. As no-one knows what alien life forms would look like, you can make them as unusual as you like. You could base them on recognizable human figures or make them completely imaginary. Here are some ideas to start you off.

Cartoon aliens

These aliens are based on the outline shapes in the box below. First copy each outline, then draw in the rest of the body. Go over the outline in black, then colour the aliens with felt tips, using a mixture of colours and patterns.

Alien from Venus

Based on what is known of the planets, you can work out the kind of features an alien might need to have in order to live on one of them.

This alien has an insulating shell to protect it from the extreme heat on Venus. On the right you can see how to get a scaly effect on the alien's body.

Drawing alien skin

Use a watercolour base for this skin. Let it dry, then draw black scales.

Use pencil crayons, leaving parts of the veins uncoloured so they look bulgy.

Use a pencil crayon base. Add scales on top in fine black or brown felt tip.

Use pencil crayons, adding hairs in brown felt tip to get a bristly effect.

Humanoid aliens

An alien might well show some physical similarities to a human being. But on a planet where conditions are different from Earth, its limbs and senses may have developed in strange ways. Here you can see some suggestions for drawing humanoid aliens.

Metal Martian

No visible ears.

All-round vision.

Four hands but only three fingers on each.

You can see how to colour the alien's skin on the opposite page. Colour its clothes with felt tips. Show shadows on its cloak by using a darker shade of the base colour.

To draw this alien, first use a pencil to copy the blue outline above on the left, then add the lines shown in orange. Fill in the shapes of the arms and legs and rub out the pencil lines inside them. Copy the alien's clothes from the main picture and draw in its features. Go over the outline in black.

In 1955, someone claimed to see a goblin-like alien peering through a farmhouse window in Kentucky, USA. It was only a metre high, with pointed ears and big, bulging eyes.

Aliens under pressure

Aliens on a low gravity planet would be tall and thin; high gravity would force aliens down into shorter, squatter shapes.

Low gravity alien

Big ears as thin air makes sounds hard to hear.

Powerfully built to lift things made very heavy by high gravity.

High gravity alien

Colour the aliens' skin using the suggestions on the opposite page.

Science fiction art

Science fiction art has become a very popular form of illustration. It is used a lot in magazines and books, and as the basis for creating special effects in films and on television. The two main types of science fiction illustration are fantasy art and comic strip art. Here you can see professional examples of both.

Fantasy art

Fantasy art shows imaginary visions of the future or other worlds. Artists often use a realistic drawing style, with unusual colours and effects to create pictures with plenty of atmosphere. Sometimes the scenes are rather frightening, but they can also be optimistic and even comic.

Fantasy artists mainly use airbrush and gouache to get subtle tones and dramatic shadows.

In this picture, the artist, Gary Mayes, uses a dramatic sky to contrast with an almost deserted planet. The loneliness of the planet is emphasized further by a single figure looking at the skeleton of a long-dead alien creature.

There are other examples of fantasy art on pages 114–117, with tips on how to create some of the professional effects.

Comic strip art

The comic strip below is a story about Dan Dare, the space hero who first appeared in Eagle magazine in 1950. The stories have been drawn by many artists, the best known being Frank Hampson and Frank Bellamy, who redesigned Dan Dare in 1960. The modern Dan Dare strip below was drawn by John Higgins for Eagle Annual in 1987.*

Short captions set the scene.

The planet is seen from an unusual viewpoint.

The background scene continues behind the whole strip.

Close-ups are mixed with longer views.

Thought and speech bubbles are often used together.

Here the reader sees the villain from the hero's viewpoint.

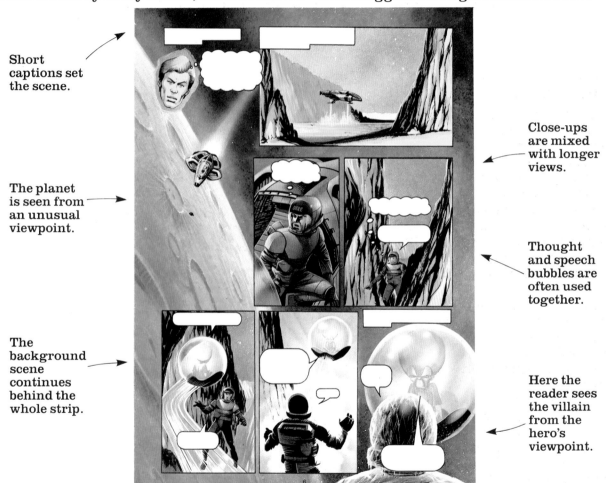

The artist credited with giving the early Dan Dare strips their distinctive look is Frank Bellamy. His way of working was unusual as, instead of sketching in pencil, he drew almost immediately in ink, using only faint, rough pencil lines as a guide. He drew in the frames after the strip was finished, sometimes using circles or zig-zags instead of box frames, or even leaving them out completely.

Drawing a comic strip

Here you can see how to build up your own science fiction comic strip, starting from a basic story idea. There are also tips for making your strip look really professional.

The plot

Start by thinking up a plot. Try and keep it quite short. Make sure the story starts off with lots of action and ends with a strong punchline.

In a comic strip, the pictures are just as important as the text. They should be action-packed and exciting to look at.

This is the plot for the comic strip on the right-hand page.

Creating characters

You need to give your characters strong personalities and draw them with slightly exaggerated features so they are easy to recognize in each frame. Here are the main characters in the comic strip on the right.

The hero

This is Captain Kovac, the hero of the story.

The villain

This is his arch-enemy, the evil Suberon.

Frames

The events in a comic strip are split into episodes and a picture is drawn for each one. These are called frames.

You can draw box rules freehand or use a ruler.

First, sketch out your ideas for each frame and draw in the boxes. You may need to try out several ideas. Add details to your sketches.

Speech bubbles

Use bubbles for spoken words, thoughts, and even sound effects. Do the lettering in capital letters to make it easy to read.

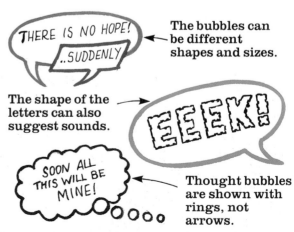

The bubbles can be different shapes and sizes.

The shape of the letters can also suggest sounds.

Thought bubbles are shown with rings, not arrows.

People read from left to right and top to bottom.

The finished strip

Here you can see how all the elements on the previous page are combined to make a comic strip. You can use the tips around the Dan Dare strip to help you make up your own

UFOs

Many people claim to have seen alien spacecraft shooting through the sky and even landing on Earth. These spacecraft are called UFOs, which stands for Unidentified Flying Objects. Some can be explained scientifically; others cannot.

UFOs come in many shapes and forms. On these pages there are just a few suggestions . . .

Flying saucers

The most common type of UFO is called a flying saucer. Not all flying saucers are saucer-shaped, though. They can also be torpedo-shaped or look like balls or spheres of light.

Use the outline shape below to help you draw a flying saucer.

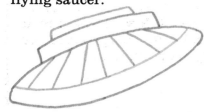

Add more details, such as windows round the side and lights underneath the body. Colour the saucer in watercolour as shown here, or in pencil crayon.

Draw the saucer bathed in a strange yellow light.

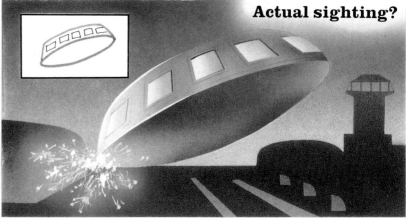

Actual sighting?

The UFO above was reported in Marseilles, France in October 1952 at 2 a.m. A pale blue light shone from its windows and sparks showered from one end. Use the outline to help you draw it.

Silhouettes and shadows

Light from behind objects.

Shadows thrown by objects.

Silhouettes are an effective way of creating an eerie look to your UFO pictures. Imagine a strong light from behind trees, spacecraft or even alien figures. Draw the outlines of the shadows in pencil, then fill in the shapes with black felt tip or ink. Make the background quite pale to give a good contrast.

Fact or fiction?

Many supposed UFOs turn out to be aeroplane lights, parachutes, kites or even low clouds.

Here you can get some ideas for drawing UFOs based on familiar objects.

An iron-shaped UFO was reported landing twice near Loch Ness, Scotland in 1971. The second time, three figures climbed on board.

Suggest the rocket fire with red and yellow shading.

Try turning a block of flats into a UFO. First draw the outline shape in the box above, then turn the windows into lights and add billowing clouds of smoke.

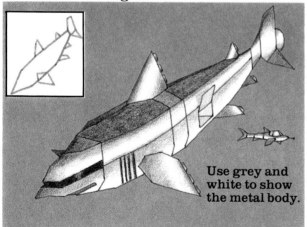

Use grey and white to show the metal body.

A shark's shape makes a good UFO. Give the basic fish shape strong angles. Use pencil crayons to colour it in.

The Tardis

In Dr Who, a famous British television programme, the Doctor flies through space in the Tardis, shown below. On the outside it looks like an old-fashioned police box but inside it is a huge time machine.*

Mix and match

Here are suggestions for some cartoon spacecraft, astronauts and aliens to add to your space scenes. Draw the aliens using different combinations of heads, bodies and legs, and add your own ideas to the spacecraft and astronauts.

Spacecraft

Using some of the basic shapes for the real spacecraft shown in this book, you can make up machines like the ones below.

Colour them any way you like and add extra details like lights, engines, wing and tail fins and smoke trails.

In the air

On the ground

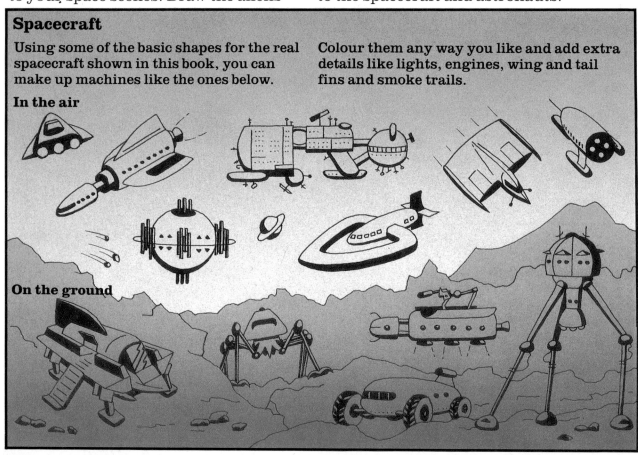

Logos

Here are some ideas for logos* to add to spacecraft, or even spacesuits. You could invent your own logos, basing the design on your initials, for example.

   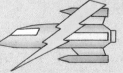

*A logo is a manufacturer's emblem.

Aliens

Heads

Bodies

Legs

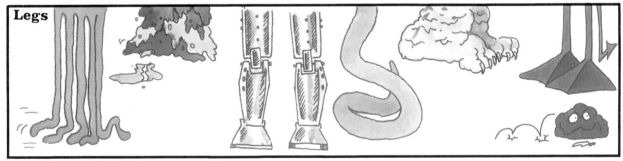

Astronauts

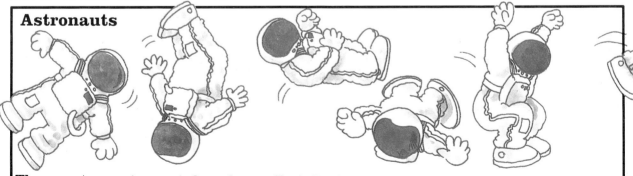

These cartoon astronauts have been affected by the low gravity on the Moon.* Draw them jumping, bouncing, or even turning somersaults in your pictures.

*See pages 112–113 for more about the Moon.

Index

The photograph on page 72 is reproduced by permission of the Syndics of the Fitzwilliam Museum, Cambridge.

First published in 1991 by Usborne Publishing Ltd, Usborne House, 83–85 Saffron Hill, London EC1N 8RT, England.

Copyright © Usborne Publishing Ltd, 1991

The name Usborne and the device   are Trade Marks of Usborne Publishing Ltd.

Printed in Belgium.